THE OCEAN'S OWN

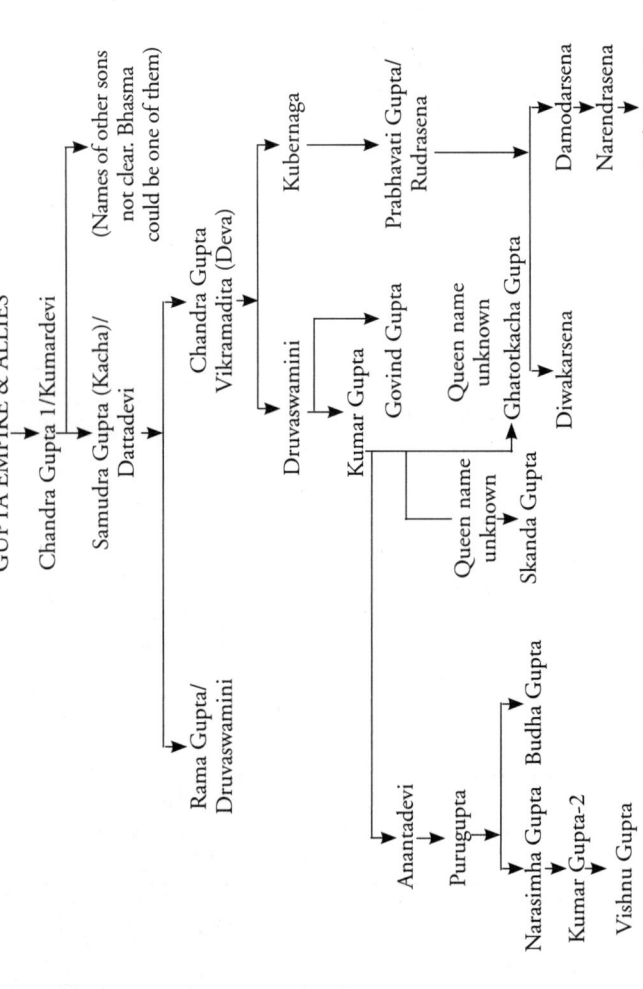

Several contemporary royal families became kinsmen to the imperial Guptas through marriage. Chandragupta I married Lichchavi princess Kumardevi, Kadamba princess Anantadevi married Kumargupta and Vakataka crown prince Rudrasena married Prabhavati Gupta. Prabhavati Gupta ruled as regent for nearly two decades and her son Damodarsena later called himself Pravarasena-II.

THE OCEAN'S OWN

NANDINI SENGUPTA

HarperCollins *Publishers* India

First published in India by
HarperCollins *Publishers* in 2021
A-75, Sector 57, Noida, Uttar Pradesh 201301, India
www.harpercollins.co.in

2 4 6 8 10 9 7 5 3 1

Copyright © Nandini Sengupta 2021

P-ISBN: 978-93-5357-965-4
E-ISBN: 978-93-5357-966-1

This is a work of fiction and all characters and incidents described in this book are the product of the author's imagination. Any resemblance to actual persons, living or dead, is entirely coincidental.

Nandini Sengupta asserts the moral right
to be identified as the author of this work.

All rights reserved. No part of this publication may be reproduced, stored in a retrieval system, or transmitted, in any form or by any means, electronic, mechanical, photocopying, recording or otherwise, without the prior permission of the publishers.

Typeset in 11/14.2 Warnock Pro at
Manipal Technologies Limited, Manipal

Printed and bound at
Thomson Press (India) Ltd.

This book is produced from independently certified FSC™ paper
to ensure responsible forest management.

To Snug and Cuddly
Because dog licks are good for time-travel

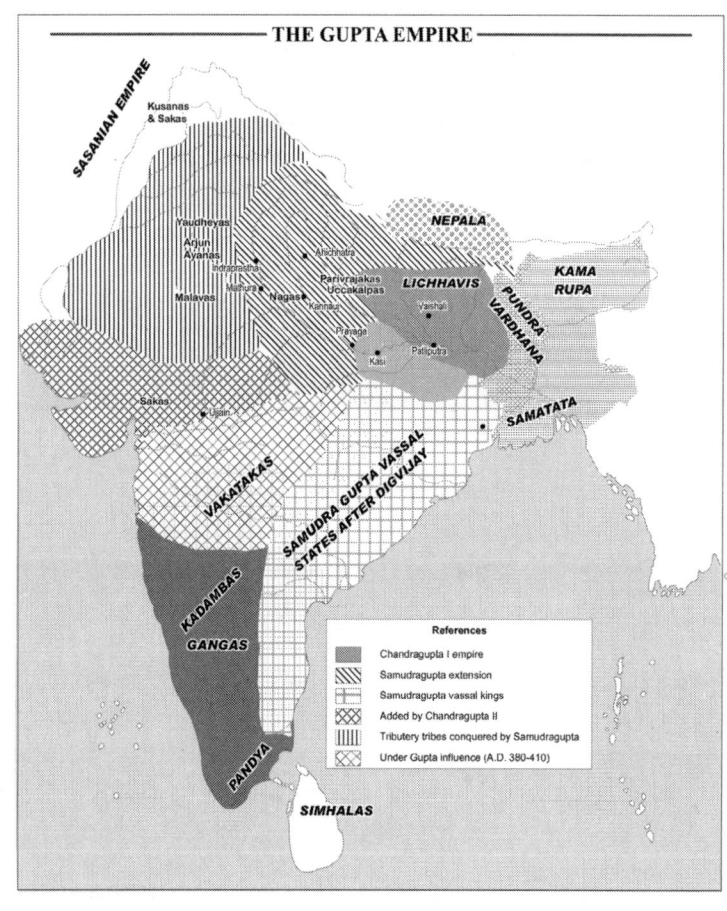

Foreword

THE ENTIRE IDEA OF *The Ocean's Own* came from the Prayag Pillar. We get most of our information about Samudragupta from his coins and the inscription or the Prayag Pillar Prasasthi by his minister, Harisena. But this incredible piece of history (which now stands in the premises of the Allahabad Fort in Prayagraj, Uttar Pradesh) carries three distinct inscriptions from three different millennia – Emperor Ashok Priyadarshi, Samrat Samudragupta and Mughal Emperor Jahangir. A wondrous time capsule, as it were, tracking three glorious epochs in India's history.

I loved the idea of this time connect, and how even what is written in stone can be lost in the mists of time. The story of the Gupta emperors was indeed lost for many centuries, even though the Gupta Age was India's 'first spring', as narrative historian Abraham Eraly described the era. At its height, the empire stretched from the Himalayas in the north to the Krishna and Godavari rivers down south, from Balkh (in Afghanistan) in the west to the Brahmaputra River in the east. It was economically prosperous, politically strong, vibrant, cosmopolitan, cultured, liberal and enlightened. However, the Gupta Emperors have, unfortunately, not received the kind of interest or patronage that turned Emperor Ashoka before them and the Mughals after into an intrinsic part of our cultural consciousness. And yet, like the other two monarchs mentioned on the Allahabad Pillar, Samudragupta was a stalwart. Often dismissed as India's Napoleon, to actually do so would be a grave injustice to this great king. Apart from being a military genius, Samudragupta was also a master administrator. It was because of rulers like him and his son Chandragupta Vikramaditya that the Gupta Empire remained as tightly knit as it did for so long, and it took more than 150 years and a thousand vicissitudes for the seams to come apart.

It's important to mention that *The Ocean's Own* is not a textbook prequel to *The King Within* (Book 1) any more than *The Poisoned Heart* (Book 2) is a typical sequel. Nor is it a textbook retelling of history. Of course, many of the characters who took centre stage in *The King Within* are introduced in this book. This includes Datta Devi, Harisena, Rama Gupta and Samudragupta himself. All these historical characters play important roles to drive the narrative throughout the trilogy, but they have been fleshed out with generous doses of creative imagination.

Like its sequels – *The King Within* and *The Poisoned Heart* – here too history rubs shoulders with fiction for the purposes of dramatic tension and storytelling. Characters like Samudragupta himself, who appears as Kacha in the story, Harisena, Datta Devi, Kumar Devi and Druvabhuti are all historical characters, but the camaraderie between the first three is entirely a product of my imagination. A word here about the use of the name 'Kacha' for Samudragupta. There is some debate among historians about the identity of the prince who was called Kacha – some say Kacha and Samudragupta are one and the same, others say Kacha was the brother who challenged Samudragupta. It is not unreasonable to assume that Samudragupta itself was an honorific title and that in his private life the king used a more intimate name.

As for the Naga relations, including Queen Padma Naga and her son Jivita, they are completely fictional but based on two historical nuggets. First, Harisena's panegyric says that when Chandragupta I announced Samudragupta's name as the heir, his brothers' faces blanched. So clearly there was some heartburn and opposition to the choice of heir, if not an open civil war. Also, Samudragupta's war against the Naga confederacy is a historical fact mentioned on the Prayag Pillar, so I put two and two together to spin this angle of a Naga usurper in his own household. The character of Bhasma is based on a reference in Arya Manjusri Mulakalpa that depicts him as the person who disputed Samudragupta's accession. There has been a fair amount of disagreement among historians about the identity of the prince who either challenged Kacha's accession or was challenged by him. But that there was some internecine trouble before Samudragupta took over is something everyone seems to agree upon. So I am hopefully on safe ground here.

The kings defeated by Kacha's grand southern campaign are all historical figures, their names, places and routes taken from the Prayag Prasasthi. However, I have added bits and pieces of fiction for the sake of drama – like Bhima is a fictional character as is Angai, even though both King Mahendra of Maha Kosala and regent Vishnugopa of Kanchi are historical figures. The details of the Silambam martial art are, of course, meticulously researched and the Pallava Dynasty's ancient link with the Nagas is also backed by documented history. Sangam classic *Manimekalai* says the first Pallava king was the offspring of the Naga princess of Manipallava and the Chola king of Killivalavan. The other reference is in the Bahur copper plate that says the Pallava ancestor Virakurcha married a Naga princess. The Bahur plates also talk about the Pallavas tracing their descent from sage Ashwathama and a Naga princess, which I have mentioned in the book.

But alongside these historical figures, I have included an entire cast of fictional characters; some central to the narrative like Princess Angai, Queen Padma Naga, Magadh Premier Brahma Deva and General Ananta Varman and others less important like General Kuber Varman, City Magistrate Devdutt, and courtesan Ragini among others. All of these are a product of my imagination but they are firmly rooted in the time and milieu that I am describing in the story. In that sense, although they are not real, they could well have been. It's just that history does not give us more detail, so I have used my imagination to fill in the gaps.

Finally, I have worked hard to ensure that the etymological references used in the story are absolutely authentic. The word *kadal kol* and the references to the sea devouring the Kanchipuram/Mammallapuram region in ancient times can be found in Sangam literature. Similarly, the Chinese pronunciation of Kusumpur/Pataliputra is taken from HH Wilson's foreword to his translation of Dandin's *Dasa Kumara Charita* where he wrote, 'That Patna was called Kusumapura, the flower city, at a late period we know from the Chinese Buddhist travelers, through whom the name Ku-su-mo-pu-lo became familiar to their countrymen.'

The Ocean's Own thus completes the Gupta Empire Trilogy and in a sense brings closure to the nine years of relentless research that backed all three books. I have lived with these characters since 2010 and now that their journey comes to a close, I feel bereft. I hope my readers will enjoy this rollicking ride through ancient India as much as I loved imagining it. I would like to thank my brother Anindya Sengupta and dear friend and author Moupia Basu for their valuable inputs on language, structure, plot, and characterization. I would like to give my little daughter Aura a big hug for all the times I have snapped at her because Kacha was facing some life-or-death dilemma that I simply had to sort out first. I would also like to thank my best friend Reshmi Dasgupta for all her support. Without her girl power backing me every step of the way, my journey as an author would not have been possible. And last, but not the least, I would like to thank my editor Rea Mukherjee for all her support and the wonderful team at HarperCollins India for their help with the manuscript. May the force be with ye all.

1
Future in the Stars

IF YOU HOLD A conch shell to your ear, you hear the roar of the waves trapped inside it. That's how I first heard the call of the ocean; long before the journey that changed my life. To the far edges of Dakshinapath, where the three oceans kiss the feet of this blessed land. Long before I met Angai, part-woman, part-wave; untamed and fierce, primal and pure, with the expanse of the sky in her eye and the tang of the salty sea on her tongue. Long before I became Parakramah Samrat Sri Samudragupta, the virtuous, the valiant, the victorious. Conqueror of kings. Emperor of Jamvudeep and all the oceans. Ruler of the world.

Yes, I am the ocean's own and here is my story.

It's been three decades, but when I look back it still feels like yesterday.

It started when father fell ill. I was then Lichchavidauhitra Kacha, the crown prince and my father's favourite son. It was the sixteenth year of his reign and my father

Maharajadhiraj Chandragupta I – who had used his vision and valour to forge an empire that stretched from Prayag to Saketa to Magadh – was on the Aryapatta throne. When I left the capital Pataliputra, he seemed in both good health and spirits. I wanted to go away on a hunting trip to Mahakantar for a few weeks with my bride, Dattadevi and best friend, Harisena. Datta and I had been affianced since childhood and grew up together under my mother Kumardevi's loving care. She knew me well; perhaps too well. Even though we were newly married, it felt sweet and familiar, like the comfort of an old quilt, soft with use and full of shared memories.

It was autumn, the season was mellow, and I was in love. We laughed and read, rode and hunted. And made love. We spent our nights gazing at the stars and dreaming of our life together. We were young and foolish – I was only twenty-five summers old, Datta a few years younger. We didn't know it then but life is not a dream. And a future written in the stars can twinkle all night but it fades away in the harsh light of daybreak.

The news came to us on one such magical evening. We'd been out hunting all day, though with Datta it was more a picnic than real blood sport. We still managed some pheasants and peacocks, and after nightfall, Harisena called out to his men and ordered them to set up camp and light a bonfire for us. With each twig thrown in, the fire crackled, its orange tips flaring upwards, greedily licking the overhanging leaves of the peepal tree under which we took refuge. The smell of slow-roasting game mixed with the fragrance of the autumn air as the sky above us turned a blaze of orange, grey and blue – a celestial palate spreading out across the horizon.

Datta curled up next to me and drew her light wool uttaria scarf around us. 'I wish we could stay here forever,' she said, smiling to herself. 'Right now, Pataliputra seems so far away, doesn't it?'

I put my arm around her and gave her a tight squeeze but said nothing. Although she grew up in the palace, Datta hated the court, with its air of intrigue and ambition. My mother had coached both of us well but with Datta, the more she learnt about politics, the less she seemed to like it. Of course, I knew in my heart that no matter how far we roamed, Pataliputra would never really be far away. It was my destiny, something I couldn't run away from. Not even for love.

As if on cue, Harisena walked up to us and sat down at the foot of the Peepal tree. Wiry, athletic and half a hand shorter than me, Harisena's frame belied his phenomenal skill as a warrior. He wasn't bulky but he was as strong as an ox, as sure-footed as a leopard, and many a joust opponent had rued their misjudgment of just how quick his sword arm could be. Crushing the cushion of dry leaves under him, Harisena stretched out and yawned. 'It's been more than two weeks but there has been no news from the palace,' he said. 'I hope there's nothing amiss.'

'Why should there be?' asked Datta, annoyed at her reverie being so rudely interrupted. 'Mother told me she would ensure we weren't disturbed unless it was a matter of life and death. And I am grateful she's kept her word.'

Harisena frowned. 'True ... but life away from court feels a bit boring after a while, doesn't it?'

'Not to me,' snapped Datta. They were nearly the same age and she loved Harisena like a brother but the two seldom agreed on anything. The only thing they had in common was their fierce love for me.

'You're feeling bereft, my friend.' I laughed. Harisena was a creature of the court and though he loved the occasional break as much as I did, politics was his lifeblood. Three weeks of hunting and picnics were simply too much leisure for him.

Harisena looked embarrassed. 'I am sorry – I should have realized how important this holiday is for the two of you.'

'When you marry, you too will realize politics can and should play second fiddle sometimes,' said Datta archly.

'Somehow, I doubt that.' I laughed.

Harisena grinned. 'But politics is far from my first love, remember? If I were to, I'd choose poetry over politics.'

This time, both Datta and I laughed out loud. 'Somehow, I doubt that too,' she said.

Our chatter was suddenly rudely interrupted by the not-too-distant sound of approaching horsemen. Harisena leapt up immediately, silently signalling for his men to lift their swords and spears. Although father's formidable administrative skills had ensured there were no significant law-and-order skirmishes, even in areas not directly under imperial command, forest tribes were notoriously difficult to control or subdue.

But the riders who burst into our campfire cocoon were not atavic tribesmen. Though covered in dust from head to toe, their leather breastplates and arm guards were clearly visible, as was the ochre-coloured imperial livery they wore underneath. These men were from Pataliputra and were clearly on some urgent mission.

The men slid off their saddles and knelt down in front of me, waiting for their leader to catch up. When he came forward, I had no doubt something had gone dreadfully wrong in the capital.

Ananta Varman was one of father's most trusted generals. I had known him from when I was a little boy and was aware of just how much my parents trusted him and depended on his friendship. In his mid-fifties, his once raven-black hair had now begun to acquire some silver highlights. However, he still looked and fought like he was fifteen years younger than he really was.

As he knelt down before me, I heard this august figure loudly and clearly pronounce the royal prasasthi, the imperial homage mandatory for not only the officers of the empire but for the palace household as well as common folk across the realm. But only the emperor was entitled to a prasasthi. No one else received it – not the queen empress or the dowager queen and certainly not a crown prince. The prasasthi could only mean one thing – a prospect too terrible for me to even contemplate. I stood there as if in a nightmare, trembling from head to foot. I couldn't think, I couldn't speak, I couldn't even breathe.

Harisena realized what was happening and quickly walked up behind me. He held me firmly by my shoulders, the pressure bringing me back to reality. 'When?' he asked simply.

'Eight days ago,' replied Ananta Varman. 'Her Majesty the queen ordered me to ride out immediately.'

'What happened?' Harisena asked.

'The affliction came suddenly,' replied Ananta Varman. 'The physicians worked through the night but couldn't save His Majesty. His last words were about you, Kumar Kacha,' he said, looking straight into my eyes. 'He said, "I have done my duty. I have chosen my tatparigrihita heir. Kacha is noble, righteous and brave. He will protect this earth and forge a destiny far more glittering than any of us could have ever imagined. I leave my legacy in his very capable hands."'

His words jolted me, cutting through my daze of disbelief. 'But he wasn't in poor health when we left him,' I muttered. 'He seemed in better spirits than I had seen in many months. So, what happened?'

Harisena, the only person close enough to hear my almost inaudible mumble, understood immediately. 'Arya Ananta Varman, was there an investigation into the emperor's sudden death? The queen and the Council of Elders are quite convinced that his death was natural, are they not?'

Ananta Varman shook his head sadly. 'I know how hard it is for Kumar Kacha to accept this sudden tragedy, but the physicians were uniformly of the opinion that his death was not caused by extraneous means. It seems he had a secret affliction of the heart and that is what caused it. He wasn't assassinated.'

'But it doesn't make sense,' I said, turning around to face Harisena. 'Do you hear me? It just doesn't make sense!'

Harisena, his hands still firmly gripping my shoulders, shook me gently. 'Snap out of it, Kacha. This is your legacy. You know it, and your father knew it. Sooner or later, you were meant to pick up the mantle. You can grieve in private but right now, you need to go forth and be an emperor.

That's what His Majesty would have expected of his tatparigrihita heir.'

I looked at my best friend through a haze of tears, the truth hitting me squarely like the deathblow of a battle axe. As long as father had occupied the Aryapatta throne, I didn't have to think about anything – I simply followed his orders. Now, I was on my own. I suddenly felt utterly alone, like when I was a little boy and had lost my way through the forest on my maiden hunt. In one fell swoop, my beautiful, unspoiled world of love and laughter had been turned on its head. The dream was over, and it was now time to face life.

The ride back to the capital seemed interminable. On we rode, through the narrow, overgrown, zigzagging forest paths that snaked through most of Mahakantar. The ruler of this wild and virgin land – Byagra Raja or the Tiger King – was an uneasy ally. Known for routine raids into neighbouring kingdoms and for an easy morality that bowed to nothing but expediency, Byagra took his time coming around to father's peace offer. But after several border skirmishes went our way, reducing both his weapon hands as well as the morale of his men, Byagra decided his adventurism was turning out to be a costly mistake. And so, a no-first-attack alliance was forged between the two kingdoms. That was five years ago. For as long as he lived, father made sure Byagra stuck to the agreement and kept himself strictly within his own boundaries. Things had even settled down enough for the Tiger King to offer a hunting vacation in

Mahakantar as a wedding gift to Datta and I – an offer father graciously accepted. But word of his death meant the mischief-maker would possibly be back to his old tricks. And capturing and ransoming the heir would suit him, perfectly, thank you very much.

Ananta Varman was aware of this risk and, under his command, had around thirty of his most capable and loyal men. Harisena had another fifty so we weren't entirely unprotected. But we still knew the danger of running into some atavic tribes armed and instigated by the Tiger King. If the raid failed and was reported back to him, he could always say he had no control over his forest folk, and that it was probably the fear of my father's formidable law enforcement next door which had kept them from running amok all this while.

Datta did not travel well. The breakneck speed of our journey back, coupled with her anxiety over what awaited us back home in Pataliputra, made it a tough ride for her. We couldn't afford to give her an ox-cart litter this time around, for fear it would slow down the entire cavalcade, thus making sitting ducks out of us. So she rode with us instead. Dressed in my turban and weapon guards, she looked like a teenage boy too young to have sprouted facial hair. Harisena joked that she was too pretty to be an imperial guard but Datta didn't rise to the bait. No one was in the mood for laughs at this point.

The first two days were uneventful. We woke at first light, rode all day with three short breaks for breakfast, lunch and dinner, and set up camp at nightfall. We slept with our weapons in our hands and our ears out for predators, animal as well as human. Although there were no signs that we were being followed – the scouts that scoured the terrain ahead and behind our train reported nothing unusual – I felt uneasy. After years of training, I had developed a sixth sense. And it was telling me to beware.

They say every battlefield, no matter how big or small, emits a certain smell. It is a queasy mix of sweat, blood and faeces as men fight, kill or empty their bowels. But to me, that nauseous odour is just the smell of fear. And it attacks the nostrils long before arms are drawn, as men lie in wait to kill and be killed. As I lay down next to the campfire that evening, I noted that queer battle smell. I knew there were attackers lurking in the shadows just outside our circle of light, waiting for the right moment to pounce.

I didn't want Datta to panic so I simply told her to lie close to me while I kept watch. Harisena immediately understood and sat down next to us, his sword unsheathed. Ananta Varman ordered his men to form a tight circle around the campfire with their shields creating a makeshift palisade around them. Everyone held on to their weapons. And waited.

They pounced on us in the darkest hour before dawn. Soft-footed and lightening-quick like leopards, guided by the last-glowing embers of a dying campfire, they entered our dugout by slitting the throats of some guards on the outer rim of the shield wall. I saw their silhouettes soundlessly pick their way through the camp in the thinning darkness and I lightly touched Harisena. I needn't have bothered though. He was ready, sword unsheathed, as was I.

We looked at each other and wordlessly signalled our move. At the count of three, I leapt up and tackled the two men closest to me. I speared the first, catching him squarely in his chest and then used his slumped body as a shield to ram into his comrade. The man lost his balance and my sword had no trouble finding his flank.

Harisena, still half-lying on the ground, used his thin knife to deftly slice the tendon on the ankle of the attacker closest to him. The man yelped and stumbled, giving Harisena the opening to rip his jugular, cleanly and nearly noiselessly. Unfortunately, the man hiccupped and fell face forward on Datta, drenching her in blood and causing her to wake up, scared and startled. Her breath knocked out by the dead weight, she pushed the body away and called out to me. I shushed her into silence immediately, but the damage had been done. The atavics knew now that we had a woman in our midst and their main body focused the attack on the three of us. The rest of our company was busy fighting off the ambush. Shields were up. Swords flashed silver in the pale grey of imminent dawn and the night air was full of gasps, grunts and the occasional death-throe scream.

I did a quick recce and realized the tribals were actually very well positioned. Ananta Varman and his core group were engaged in fierce combat near the shield wall. The attackers had surrounded us well enough to cut off any immediate assistance from that side. I threw Datta her sword, signalling to her to get behind me. Harisena took the cue and backed in too, forming a tight three-pointed star, a classic defensive position. A casual look told me there were at least thirty men surrounding us. I knew these forest tribesmen were no match for our seasoned swordplay, but what I was worried about were their archers. Atavic tribals typically dipped their arrowheads in poison – mostly hemlock juice. If they were to let loose their arrows, we would have to defend with our shields first. Which means fighting with a handicap.

'Harisena, disable the archers first,' I whispered. 'From what I can see, there are five of them amongst this rabble. You can spot them from the quivers slung across their backs.'

Harisena nodded. He kept an assortment of thin knives tucked into his breastplate and arm guards. The tribals knew our archers were cut off from us, which meant they weren't expecting an aerial assault.

Harisena was lightening quick – in a smooth, fluid motion he plucked out the knives from his breastplate and hurled them in the direction of the two archers facing him. I heard the men hiccup and slump forward – their comrades gibbered in their strange tongue, too astonished to comprehend what had happened – and I knew my friend had found his target. Harisena slipped one knife into my hand and I hurled, cutting down the archer in front of me who was about to shoot his first arrow. Rattled, the atavics decided to dump their arrows and swamp us with their sheer numbers instead. Exactly as I had expected they would do.

I knew Harisena and I were enough to take on this semi-trained rabble in a clean swordfight, and Datta was well-trained enough to defend herself too. 'Don't break this formation,' I whispered into her ear and unsheathed both my Khadga broadsword and my trusted Asi. Behind me, I heard a faint rustle that told me Harisena had drawn his weapons too. Like me, he could use both his arms, a

Parashu battle axe in his left hand to hack his way through and the Asi in his right to cut down the enemy.

'Harisena, NOW,' I shouted, just as the tribals started closing in on us, their ululating battle cry catching the attention of Ananta Varman. The half-light did them no favours – I caught the first two easily, decapitating one with a mighty swing of the Khadga and disemboweling the other with a clean swipe of the Asi.

'Kacha, don't bother about protecting my flank – I can defend myself,' shouted Datta. 'Take them down before the surprise wears off.'

I nodded in agreement, and Harisena and I split up to run headlong into the two halves of the tribal attack. Although good at ambushes, the tribals had never faced the kind of lightening quick swordplay that my weapons master insisted was my special forte. Their weapons too were crude – bows and arrows, clubs and spears. They had nothing to face the challenge of a beautifully made and meticulously sharpened Asi edge. Their heavier weapons made them slow and they had no idea what they were up against. This wasn't hard work for me – hack, hack, slash, slash – I wielded my Khadga and Asi with as much speed as I could muster, creating panic and confusion amongst their ranks. From the screams and grunts behind me, I knew Harisena was doing the same thing. The tribals fought bravely but heavy weapons are difficult to control and wield with precision, so their blows seldom hit home. Nearly an hour later, I had eight dead and two gravely injured men at my feet. I turned around to find Harisena fighting off the few remnants of his group. Only six of the initial band of thirty now remained, and they were busy retreating. Datta stood with her sword unsheathed but was protected by a circle of Ananta Varman's guards. The ululations of the tribals as they had rushed in on us caught the commander's attention and he'd immediately sent some men across to protect the crown princess.

Near the shield wall too, the fight was wrapping up as the tribals stepped back, looking for forest cover to retreat. The attack didn't go well for them. A quick look around told me we'd taken down three quarters of the attacking atavic force. Still, Ananta Varman wanted to take no chances. 'Decapitate all the dead and injured and put their heads up on stakes,' he barked out a command. I didn't much care for this brutal display, but I held my tongue. We were still in enemy land and this would send out a strong signal to Byagra should he have any other ideas.

Harisena walked up to me, drenched in sweat despite the chill of the late-October dawn. Still breathing heavily from his exertion and the adrenalin rush of a close combat, he looked me in the eye and said, 'This is just the beginning. There'll be many more, Kacha. Make no mistake.'

'I know,' I replied. 'I am ready.'

2

Snakes and Ladders

THE REST OF THE ride back to Pataliputra threw no more surprises our way. Clearly, Ananta Varman's brutal message had hit home and the atavic tribesmen we met along the remainder of our journey were mostly harmless. Some of them were, in fact, quite helpful, offering our scouts details of the route along with game and fodder for the way.

I had plenty of time to think things through as we rode on in companionable silence. Both Datta and Harisena sensed my mood and let me be, leaving me alone with my thoughts for a while. I was still trying to come to terms with father's death and what that would mean for me, as well as my family. I wasn't unprepared for the job – ever since he crowned me his tatparigrihita heir three years ago, father had been training me for this very day. It started with me attending court regularly for just over a year, followed by a ten-month stint across the provinces looking into law and order and taxation issues, and another eight months visiting our ally kingdoms to suss out anything that might have been brewing in the neighbourhood. I was ready for my destiny and father's last words convinced me that he knew it too.

What I was worried about was my own backyard. Court politics was nothing new to me. I grew up listening to my parents discussing Chanakyaniti and ever since my eighteenth year, I was allowed to sit in when the Council of Twelve Elders met. But my first year as a courtier, after being anointed heir apparent, was an eye-opener. I realized it was one thing to be a fly on the wall when you had no stake in the game. But quite another when the rest of the pit saw you as both predator and prey. Harisena's response was to immediately put into place a network of informants and supporters, both in court as well as inside the palace. 'Knowledge is power,' he told me. 'We need to know what's going on so we can always be ready for surprises. To be unprepared is to sign your own death warrant.'

Apart from Harisena's network, I also had my mother and her Lichchavi kinsmen as fall-back options. Strong, sharp and armed with a steely will, my mother could be both a formidable friend and an implacable enemy. Unlike most women in the imperial household, she liked to keep herself both informed and invested in what was going on in the kingdom. She had her Lichchavi relations to back her up in court and she had father's ear. Mother was not just a ceremonial figurehead; she was literally the second-most powerful person in court. And having her on my side was my biggest advantage.

My father's household wasn't as elaborate as many of our ally kingdoms but it still included several minor wives acquired as a result of his neighbourhood diplomacy policies. As the Patta Mahadevi, mother outranked all of these queens, and it was her skill in handling people and power that kept these often-warring factions quiet, at least outwardly. But resentments bubbled under the surface, venom that I now expected to spill out into the open.

Indeed, among the confused jumble of anguish, anger and apprehension with which I tried to make sense of my new reality, one thing kept nagging me: the sudden attack by atavic tribesmen was too convenient for Byagra to just be a coincidence. He'd clearly ordered his irregulars to attack because he knew there was a power vacuum in Pataliputra. But the question is, how did he know so quickly? And before I did?

This is what I asked Harisena when we set up camp that evening. As usual, my friend told me, rather frankly, what I was trying not to admit to myself; at least not without proof. 'There is only one possibility – Byagra knows the news about His Majesty because he has a mole in the palace in Pataliputra. A mole that is close enough to the royal family to be privy to this important piece of information. And I think both you and I know who that is.'

I kept quiet, not wanting my ugly suspicion to be so rudely confirmed. 'This is just conjecture,' I said, almost to myself. 'There's no proof.'

Datta, who was sitting close by and hugging herself tightly against the evening chill, looked up and caught my eye. 'I know you bear your half-brothers no ill will Kacha,' she said softly, 'but you also know who you can and cannot trust. I have too much faith in your intelligence to believe otherwise.'

Harisena nodded. 'Remember what happened when the emperor anointed you his tatparigrihita heir? I was standing right behind His Majesty, facing you and the Council of Twelve Elders. Bhasma's face was like a mirror to his soul – dark with the rage of unfulfilled desire.'

'And he's not the only one,' added Datta. 'I saw the way Jivita's face clouded over when father called you the noblest of his sons. They are all your enemies, Kacha, because you have what they all desire.'

I closed my eyes, not wanting to believe my worst suspicion. Almost the same age, Bhasma and I were rivals from the time we were old enough to realize how tangled our futures were. In the weapons room, he excelled with the Tomara iron club while my forte was swordplay. Born of different mothers, we grew up natural adversaries, both vying for father's attention and approval in weapons' training as well as at our gurukul classwork. Father loved us both equally, leading Bhasma to believe his claim to the throne was no less than mine, even though his mother was not the Patta Mahadevi queen empress. A minor Naga princess who was married off to my father as a peace offering, Bhasma's mother Padmanaga brought neither men nor land as her dowry. Perennially overshadowed by my mother, Lichchavi-Princess Kumardevi, thanks to the importance that her family and clan enjoyed in court, Padma deeply resented her rival's pre-eminence. Not only was my mother the Queen Empress, but father also treated her as his equal in all respects. I proudly call myself 'Lichchavidauhitra' and father routinely minted coins which had both his and my mother's likeness imprinted on them.

That, I suspected, was the reason Bhasma and Jivita grew up as messed up as they did. Padma transferred all her bitterness to her two sons, egging them on so they would get what she never did – father's affection and the assurance that they came first. Not physically strong, Jivita was not particularly interested in weapons training. But he was the brain behind most of the schemes the two brothers hatched to take me on. Like the hemlock juice-laced Madhvi fruit cocktail I was served during the Vasant Utsav spring festival two years ago. Thankfully, I noticed there was something amiss with the taste. So I took no more than a mouthful or two, even though I was thirsty. Still, I became violently ill later that evening. However, thanks to my mother's care and the court physician's potions, I recovered completely in a few days.

Harisena had no doubt the brothers were behind this poisoning but when we took our suspicion up to father, he refused to believe it. 'They were not even in the capital when this happened,' he told me. 'I know you boys don't get along sometimes, but I don't think my sons would try to poison one another. Don't think the worst of them, Kacha. They are, at the end of the day, still your blood brothers. And it's best not to breed enemies in your own household.'

I couldn't argue with father, so I held my tongue. I knew why he said what he did – although my rivalry with Bhasma and Jivita had begun to acquire a nasty hue long before this incident, neither brother ever stepped out of line in father's presence. They knew better.

Privately though, Harisena, Datta and I had our doubts. I had been openly mocked in public, viciously attacked during weapons practice, and ambushed on my morning horse-riding exercises outside the city. Jivita had even tried to bend father's ear about how I was being led astray by Harisena. On this particular occasion, it was my mother's intervention that prevented my best friend from being banished from the palace.

To his credit, father remained determinedly unbiased all through our growing-up years. His children were given equal attention and opportunity to prove themselves. I got along well with most of my other half-brothers and sisters, even though Harisena and Datta were not very sure if the bonhomie was real or purely for my father's benefit. But Bhasma and Jivita made no attempt to hide their hatred and resentment, often comparing the political and military heft of their maternal relations – the Naga kings of northern Panchal and Padmavati – with the Lichchavis, wondering what would happen if the Nagas formed a confederacy against the empire.

'My mother is related to King Achyuta of Ahichhatra on her father's side and King Nagasena of Padmavati on her mother's side,' Bhasma once said, during one of our many altercations. 'If she wanted, she could have shown those arse-licking Lichchavis whose support is really holding this kingdom aloft. But she loves father too much to hurt him. He should know that and respect her for it.'

'Achyuta and Nagasena are our vassals, not equals,' I had shot back. 'If they raise their hoods, father will break their backs this time. Remember, they asked for father's protection with a marriage alliance, not the other way around.'

'That's not true,' Jivita butted in. 'They accept father as overlord because they love and respect him as kinsman.'

'And there are other Naga kingdoms that don't bend their knee to the empire of Magadh,' shouted Bhasma, his pallid face red with rage. 'If push comes to shove, all the Nagas will have each other's back.'

'That's treason, you know,' I replied calmly. 'If I tell father, you and your precious Naga relations will be in trouble, brother.'

That threat always worked like a charm, and this time was no exception. Jivita pulled his brother away, furiously scolding him under his breath. 'That's quite enough. Come away before you make an even bigger fool of yourself.'

The fight had fizzled out for the day, but Bhasma's outburst gave me something to think about. I realized that the only thing keeping our Naga relations at bay was the fear of father's sword. As his successor, I knew not to enjoy that luxury till I proved myself on the battlefield.

That memory now came back to haunt me. I knew my half-brothers were very close to their Naga relations, including distant cousin Ganapati Naga, ruler of Mathura. If Byagra, whose territory is more than a week's ride from Pataliputra, already knew about father's death, the Naga kings had to know too because it would be in Bhasma's interest to inform as many alliance rulers as possible. If they were to rebel, it would be good for him. After all, it's always easier to fish in troubled waters.

I looked up to the sky, trying to see if my future – the real one, not what Datta and I dreamt up – was still written in the stars. *Don't grieve now*, I told myself. *If you allow yourself to break down, your legacy will be snatched away from you and you will have let father down. Let the world know what Lichchavidauhitra Kacha can do. Unsheathe your sword, and destroy all those who stand between you and your destiny. Uproot them. Obliterate them. Purge your world of them.*

Mother, I am coming home.

On the ninth day, we reached the outskirts of Pataliputra. From a distance, we could see that the capital's enormous, spiked, wood-and-iron gates were closed, and there were soldiers patrolling the ramparts of the fort. I saw the imperial Garuda Dwaja pennant fluttering gaily from the palace tower in the mellow golden sunshine, untouched by the tragedy and the uncertainty that tainted this gorgeous autumn morning. The jetty on the River Ganga – usually crowded with boats ferrying everything from flowers to Roman Sura wine to the capital – was curiously empty but for a posse of liveried guards, their ochre uniforms clearly visible despite the distance. The guards stood with their weapons drawn, ready to strike at the slightest provocation. Clearly, the city was watching its back.

As a precaution, Ananta Varman decided to split our party up. Harisena and a handful of our men rode on towards the city to recce the situation. If all were well, he would send word for us to follow before mid-day. We had to wait for their signal and escape quickly should things not go as planned. 'I know you are anxious to see your mother, but it is better to be safe,' said Ananta Varman, apologetically. 'So many things could have changed in these two weeks that I have been away.'

I nodded in agreement. We had no way of knowing if Bhasma, Jivita and their band of Naga sympathizers had already usurped power. We didn't know if mother was all right, or under house arrest of some sort. Riding in without any information would have been foolhardy. So we kept our weapons handy and waited for Harisena's signal. It seemed an endless wait but just before the noon prahar gong, we saw the signal we were waiting for – my tiger pennant being hoisted alongside the Garuda Dhwaja. Almost immediately, we heard the trumpets from the watch towers blow their welcome as the city doors creaked open, bit by bit, revealing a company of palace guards led by Harisena.

Looking back, I can recall that ride back home as vividly as if it were just yesterday. I remember every small, insignificant detail – the bright golden yellow of the turmeric-smeared rice that people showered on us in fistfuls. The fragrance of the champak garlands mixed with the heady smell of wet earth, as the women sprinkled water on our path to settle the dust. The roar of greeting that rose from the crowds lining up alongside the wide brick-and-mud-baked thoroughfare, leading up from the main gates into the palace complex at the heart of the city. The skyline gleaming with its row of copper urns adorning the doorways of prominent noblemen. The vermilion and turmeric wall paintings depicting everything from Vishnu's conch shell to ears of rice, Laxmi's footprints and the swastika symbol. Little children playing hop scotch beside the road. Rows of shops selling betel leaf and areca nuts, beads and bangles, sweetmeats and salty spiced yogurt shakes. All the excited voices. The combined cacophony of kettledrums, town criers and the clop-clop of horse hooves ... every sound and sight remain seared in my mind's eye to this day. I remember drinking it all in greedily as my heart swelled ... I was never more in love with Pataliputra. This rambling, brick-laid city of princes and paupers, aspirations and avarice, virtue and venom, was more than my home. It was my destiny. And I knew in that moment, no matter how many times I lost my heart, Pataliputra would always claim it back.

Our cavalcade took the better part of an hour to reach the palace as we stopped again and again on our way to accept water, sweetmeats and flowers. We were greeted at the palace gates by the Twelve Elders and my half-brothers, Bhasma and Jivita. 'Welcome home, Kumar Kacha,' said Brahma Deva, the senior-most member of the Council of Elders and one of mother's biggest supporters in court. 'I know how difficult these past few weeks have been for you. But as heartbroken as you are, this is the time you will need to put all your personal concerns aside, and take up the responsibility your father has entrusted to you. The Aryapatta throne awaits you, Lichchavidauhitra Kacha. The sooner we have the coronation ceremony, the better it is for this realm.'

I nodded in agreement, even though every bone in my body was aching to meet my mother first. 'I am at your disposal,' I replied. 'All I ask is that I be allowed to meet my mother first.'

Brahma Deva stepped aside, allowing Datta and me to walk right through to the antarmahal, the private living quarters of the imperial household. I broke into a jog and ran down the long corridor – with its fresco-painted sandstone ceiling and carved sandalwood pillars – with Datta close behind me. As the queen empress, mother occupied the entire western wing of the palace overlooking the Sonbhadra, the second of the two rivers that form a natural moat around the capital. As I walked in through the silver inlaid doors leading to her private wing, the sweet fragrance of jasmine blossoms wafted in. Mother loved those tiny white flowers and every window in her part of the palace was overgrown with Jasmine creepers.

I found her in her favourite spot: an airy colonnade overlooking the river where she liked to spend most of her private time. I am not sure what I was expecting but when Datta and I entered the room, we were greeted with a scene almost breathtakingly routine. Mother was seated on a low wooden stool, going through what looked like the household expense ledger. Her two ladies-in-waiting sat at her feet, threading a heap of white-and-orange coral jasmine flowers into an intricate garland. She looked up as we walked in and opened her arms to us. Datta and I walked into the tight familiar hug, our biggest comfort and refuge all through childhood and adolescence. 'It's all right, my children,' she whispered. 'Welcome home.'

I pulled away and looked into her eyes. Suddenly, I knew how wrong I was to think nothing had changed. Nothing gave away the tempest raging inside her, except that close-set, piercing gaze. Not the tangled hair, unoiled, uncombed and untied in mourning. Not the rough white sari, wrapped tightly to fend off the autumn nip. Not even the bare neck, wrist, arms and ears. It was never easy to hold her stare. When Queen Empress Kumardevi looked into your eyes, she could see your soul. The only time that gaze softened was when she smiled, which wasn't often. Now, when she looked at Datta and I, she seemed to be willing herself to smile. When she finally did, it did not reach her eyes.

'I stayed alive so I could hold the two of you to my heart one more time,' she said, softly. 'My children, get ready to fight the enemies within.'

Datta frowned. 'I do not understand, mother,' she said simply.

'Padma tried her best to make me accompany your father on his funeral pyre. She said as the Patta Mahadevi, it was both my duty and privilege.'

My grip tightened on her slender arms. My tongue went dry. A vein throbbed uncontrollably at my temples and I felt dizzy with anger and fear.

'How dare she,' I said, through gritted teeth.

'Well, half the council agreed with her actually,' said mother, her voice strangely matter-of-fact and devoid of emotion. 'Piety can sometimes be an excellent cover for perfidy.'

I could feel Datta trembling next to me, but mother didn't seem to notice. 'They even tried to anoint Bhasma the interim crown prince in your absence,' she said, turning her unflinching gaze towards me. 'His Majesty was too ill to command otherwise and the Nagas suddenly became very vocal in court.'

'Why didn't you send word?' asked Datta. 'We could have come back earlier.'

'I gave you my word that I wouldn't disturb the two of you unless it was a matter of life and death,' mother replied. 'I waited till it was.'

Datta gave me a sidelong glance and I saw nothing but regret in her large, tear-stained eyes.

'What about our Lichchavi cousins?' I asked.

'Thank god for them,' replied mother. 'They sent for reinforcements the moment your father fell ill, and in court Brahma Deva and my other friends rallied around me. The Council was almost evenly divided but the matter was decided when Brahma Deva produced a letter your father had written to him many years ago. "Should I die before her, let Kumardevi continue as she always has," he had written. "She's Magadh's Kula Lakshmi. I am what I am because she's by my side. The empire will thrive under her guidance."'

A shiver ran down my spine. I realized just how close I had come to losing both my parents and my future. 'How do things stand now?' I asked.

'The Lichchavi reinforcements have arrived so the Nagas are outnumbered and quiet,' replied mother. 'But your brothers won't stop plotting against you, Kacha. You need to get your bearings right and ready your weapon arm as quickly as possible. Make no mistake, son – your coronation won't go unchallenged.'

Our conversation was rudely interrupted as Harisena burst into the room. He knelt down before us and said, his voice quivering with anger and agitation, 'I bear bad news. A Naga confederacy is planning to rebel against Magadh. My spies have just brought me the news.'

'What is a Naga confederacy?' asked Datta, not able to wrap her head around this latest sling of fortune.

'What he means is that Naga kings, Achyuta of Ahichhatra, Nagasena of Padmavati and Ganapati Naga of Mathura have joined forces,' I explained, suddenly feeling calm. 'May be others too.'

'They are coming for us,' said Harisena.

'They are coming for me,' I replied.

3

Throne of Blood

LOOKING BACK, DATTA ALWAYS says she remembers very little of the coronation week. For her, it was one big blur. Not for me though. I remember every detail of those nail-biting days. Those long meetings which stretched well into the night. The twice-a-day updates from our network of spies. The anxiety. The suspense. The nervous tension in the air. And through it all, my mother's piercing gaze, unwavering in its faith in my ability to rise above anything and everything that came my way.

In a sense, it all began when Harisena burst in with the news of the Naga uprising. I saw mother's eyes flash with fury. Datta looked stunned and Harisena seemed flushed with adrenalin. I should have felt that same battle rush, except I didn't. The uncertainties and apprehensions of the past two weeks suddenly melted away. The Naga rebellion gave me clarity – now I knew what I had to do and how I had to do it.

The first test was the meeting of the Council of Elders and the entire royal family the next morning. 'Bhasma will have his supporters stake their claim on his behalf – make no mistake,' said mother.

'Then we must create enough confusion to throw their plans into disarray,' I said.

'How will you do that?' asked Datta, still a bit dazed at how quickly things were moving.

Harisena and I exchanged a quick glance. Then he smiled. 'We have to tell them that we will be in two places at the same time.'

'How's that possible?' asked mother, her brow creased in a deep frown. 'This is no time for childish pranks.'

'It's no prank, mother,' I assured her. 'If we can pull this off, my coronation will go through without a murmur.'

Mother didn't look particularly convinced. 'So what do you boys have in mind?'

'The Chakrapani Vishnu temple in the outskirts of the capital,' I said. 'Before coronation, the emperor-elect and his queen normally ride out to pray in this sanctum. I shall tell the Council of Elders that Datta and I intend to go there this evening so that the coronation can take place immediately after the council meeting tomorrow morning.'

'You do realize that route is lonely and perfect for an ambush?' asked mother.

'I do.' I smiled at her. 'I know Bhasma and his cronies will not want to miss out on a chance like this.'

Harisena's eyes lit up as he understood my plan. 'I will dress up like a woman and take my place beside Kacha instead of Datta,' he said. 'A handful of my best men can wear their gaudiest veils to pass off as ladies-in-waiting.'

'You're offering yourself as bait?' asked mother, her voice sounding shrill with alarm.

'Yes,' I replied. 'That's the only way to draw them out.'

'But how do you know Bhasma will be there too?' asked Datta. 'He could well send in his henchmen to take you out.'

'Simple,' I replied. 'I shall invite him to ride out with me. If he's as cocksure of being chosen the emperor-elect as I think he is, thanks to the Naga rebellion, he'll come. He won't allow a small thing like that to delay his coronation tomorrow.'

As we rode out in silence, I stole a glance at Bhasma. His face was bony and pale, like his mother's. With his hooded eyes and thin lips, he looked not unlike a serpent himself, even though the women in court fancied him the handsomer of the two of us. I couldn't believe how easy it was to draw him out. 'Tomorrow will decide our fate – yours and mine,' I had told him. 'But the coronation cannot happen unless we do a full fire sacrifice at the Chakrapani temple. I am going this evening. You can come if you want to.'

'Wouldn't miss it for the world,' he sneered. 'But you do know that you're not allowed arms or guards when you go to the temple?' he asked.

'Of course; Datta and I shall go unarmed and alone except for a few of her ladies-in-waiting.'

Secretly, I was thankful Jivita was not around to suspect foul play. Imperious and arrogant, Bhasma fancied himself much more than all the girls who fancied him. But for all his bravado and skill with the Tomara iron club, he was still easy to read. It was his mother and younger brother who did most of the plotting; Bhasma was too busy brawling to be interested in the realpolitik of Chanakyaniti. Mother called him a fool but I found him bitter and bumptious, but blunt. With Bhasma, what you saw was what you got.

Looking away, I glanced at Harisena riding beside me in a demurely covered litter. His lithe, athletic frame was wrapped in a bundle in Datta's heavy gold-bordered red uttaria veil that covered his head and fell well below his face. He didn't look particularly ladylike to me – his only concession was to shave off his thin moustache and paint his lips with betel juice. Indeed, his distinctly unfeminine feet – hairy toes, unseemly bunions and all – sticking out from under the white antariya sari were a dead giveaway. Still, Bhasma seemed too wrapped up in his own thoughts to notice, which was a blessing. I wasn't carrying any arms myself, except a long, sharp jewel pin tucked in my cummerbund. Harisena and his men-in-disguise were, of course, carrying knives and swords hidden in the voluminous folds of their saris.

Our ambush point was just short of the large boulders at the base of a small hillock on which the temple stood. Apart from the bramble dotting this bleak landscape, there was little vegetation cover on the hillside or along the 400-steps cut into the rock face that led up to the temple. It was a lonely stretch. There was light forest cover on the right of the mud track road, a mere 100 paces away. Close enough for a tactical retreat if needed, yet allowing enough clean ground for an open sword fight. The left was a sheer craggy rock face, so we were safe from any attack on that side. Most importantly, the spot was too far away from the hilltop temple for the priests to notice any scuffle. It was perfect.

Our enemies clearly thought so too for the attack came just as we reached the boulders. A hail of arrows from the bramble bushes that sprouted between those giant prehistoric rocks made us duck for cover. Almost immediately, Harisena's guards threw off their scarves and unsheathed their swords. I saw surprise in Bhasma's eyes – the fool actually thought his ambush would go unchallenged. We were riding side by side, so my first reaction was to grab the reins of his horse. Before he could react, I had wrapped one arm around his neck in a stranglehold and pulled him over onto my horse. Holding him in a death grip, I pulled out the long jewel pin from my cummerbund and dug its tip into his belly. 'It's just a jewel pin,' he laughed nervously.'

'It's poisoned,' I replied. 'Tell your friends to back off or I'll dig this in. Do it NOW.'

'You can't kill me brother, I am a prince of the blood,' he sneered. 'And even if you do, my friends won't let you live either. Though I must say you're smarter than I thought. Still, you and your men are horribly outnumbered. And you're not carrying your long bows either. What a pity.'

'Save your swagger,' I hissed into his ear. 'Call off the archers or I will use you as my shield.'

I slid off the horse, pulling him down with me to drive home my threat. Still holding him in an arm grip in front of me, I started walking towards the bramble cover from where the archers were shooting. 'Stop shooting or risk killing your prince,' I shouted. 'You want to fight, come out and fight with your swords.'

The threat worked. Unless exceptionally skilled, archers aren't particularly accurate with their aim. There's a reason why Arjun was as venerated in the Mahabharata as he was. The eye and the strength needed for that kind of precision is rare. Typically, archers let loose a volley, hoping that their arrows will find some targets. It's a hit or miss game, and having a live shield made it an impossible game to win.

The Nagas realized this too and the arrow shower stopped. Harisena and four of his men quickly formed a tight circle around me even as a group of armed riders burst out of the thin forest cover on the right. I was hoping I had something more substantial to defend myself with than a poisoned jewel pin. Luckily, Harisena seemed to have read my mind and just as the Naga charge galloped upon us, he thrust a sword into my free hand and I let the pin fall to the ground.

I held the sword blade to Bhasma's belly and used my arm grip around his neck to move back towards the rock face. I needed to protect my back while Harisena and his men took on the Naga riders. Bhasma tried to wriggle out of my sword-and-strangle embrace but it was no good. I'd learnt this trick during wrestling practice and it always came in handy during face-to-face combat. 'Move and I slice your belly open,' I whispered in his ear. Bhasma was almost gagging but the pressure of the sword blade on his stomach made him stop thrashing about. This gave me time to look around and take in the fight.

There were around twenty-five armed riders, while the archers still waited behind the bushes to let loose should Bhasma manage to break free. Harisena had around ten of his best men so I thought it was an even fight. I saw

Harisena's Parashu battle-axe swiftly decapitate one Naga soldier while he buried his sword into the breast of another, slicing smoothly through the leather breastplate as if it were made of butter. The Nagas thought riding into our party would help scatter the guards but that was a mistake. Harisena's men crouched at ground level and aimed their strikes at the horses, reducing men and beast to a howling heap on the blood-soaked mud track. After that it was easy picking. They made an incongruous picture, these sari-clad men, their eyes wild with blood lust, hacking, slashing, spearing their way through the enemy ranks. The Nagas fought bravely but they were simply out-skilled and out-maneuvered by the more battle-hardened and better-trained imperial guards. They fought like fiends cutting down horse and man with such lightening speed that the archers lost their nerve and started their volleys again. This was my cue to walk back into the battle arena, now slippery with spilled blood, brain and faeces. All around there were men writhing, groaning and screaming for the deliverance of death. One trying to stop the gushing blood from his slit abdomen which spilled out most of his intestines as well, one stuffing his uttaria scarf on a bloody hole where an eye had been, while another slumped on the ground too stunned to realize his weapon arm had been hacked off.

I could feel Bhasma shivering – he'd not expected the ambush to go so wrong. I walked him carefully, one step at a time, to face the bramble-strewn boulders. 'Stop shooting,' I shouted. 'If your arrows kill Prince Bhasma, my men will hunt you down. And you will be flayed alive in the palace square.'

The arrow shower stopped once again and this time Harisena spoke up. 'Go back to whoever sent you. Tell them we hold Prince Bhasma. We will do with him as Kumar Kacha deems fit. GO. NOW.'

It was almost midnight when I reached the palace. I knew mother would be waiting for news, and when I walked into her bedchamber I was thankful there were no ladies-in-waiting around. She was sitting on the floor, reading some scrolls by the light of a single lamp. She looked up as I came in. I saw relief flood her eyes as she held out her arms to me. 'I was so afraid,' she said softly.

'Don't be,' I told her. 'We have him.'

'Where?'

'Harisena is holding Bhasma in a cave near the Chakrapani temple,' I told her. 'He and his men will hide Bhasma there till the coronation is over.'

Mother nodded. 'I can tell you now, I didn't think this wild plan of yours would really work.'

I smiled. 'We need to talk to our Lichchavi relations,' I told her, 'first thing tomorrow morning. Before the council meeting.'

Mother smiled back. 'I have asked my cousin Narasimha and Brahma Deva to come over at dawn. They will be here at first light.'

In the heat of the skirmish that evening, I had forgotten just how resourceful mother was. 'Of course, you did,' I told her, smiling. 'Serves me right for trying to tell you what to do.'

I retired to my own bedchamber, both bone tired and feverishly excited. My limbs weighed like rocks and my head throbbed but I couldn't sleep. I was worried about how things would go at the Council meeting, and the battle rush meant I was on a nervous high, reliving the encounter of the evening. I knew Harisena could not hold Bhasma for more than half a day. Any longer, and tongues would start wagging at court. My plan was to simply say that he and I had been attacked by Naga soldiers on the way to the Chakrapani temple the evening before and that I lost him in the melee. I had already ordered reinforcements for Harisena so he could fend off any further Naga incursions till noon. The idea was to hold our prisoner till then, by which time the coronation and anointment would hopefully be over. That is, if all went according to plan.

I had given Harisena strict instructions to ride out towards Mathura immediately after releasing Bhasma for I knew Bhasma would name him as his captor when he returned to the palace. He wouldn't be able name me, the anointed emperor, without being punished for treason so he would blame everything on Harisena. An attack on a member of the royal family merits a painful death on the impaling stake. The only way I could disprove Bhasma's allegations was if I announced in court that I had already dispatched Harisena and his men to scout out the Naga campaign. I needed some senior courtiers and elders to back up my claim; hence the dawn meeting with Brahma Deva and Narasimha.

I weighed the pros and cons over and over again as I waited for daybreak. Beside me, Datta slept, her serene forehead furrowing with frown lines now and then, as if she was thinking hard in her dreams. I snuggled up to her, my nostrils full of her jasmine and sweat smell, scared of losing my way if I pulled away from her then. I buried my face into the mass of ringlets that spread out like a fan around her head, crushed jasmine sprigs still enmeshed in them. They reminded me of Datta as a little girl, trailing behind Harisena and me, her small serious face framed by a profusion of curls that no amount of oil could ever fully tame. Consort, confidante, companion, then as now, all I wanted was to protect this fragile being who trusted me blindly with every bone in her body. And now, I was gambling with her future as well as my own. For her sake and mine, I had to win. *Tomorrow*, I kept repeating in my head. *Tomorrow all of this will be over. Tomorrow will be a new day.*

It was a promise, both to her and to myself.

The council meeting began early. It was a full house with all Twelve Elders, senior generals in the imperial army as well as the entire royal household attending. I saw my stepmother Padmanaga sitting right in front with Jivita at her elbow. Mother was there too, as was Datta who looked just a little bit frightened by the enormity of it all. I hoped and prayed Brahma Deva and Narasimha had done what they'd promised to do – ask Ananta Varman to speak to the generals, and meet as many council members loyal to mother as they could. After the mandatory invocation to Lord Vishnu, Brahma Deva began the proceedings. 'My friends,' he said, 'we are here today to announce the appointment of Prince Kacha as the emperor elect. As you must have heard, there is a Naga insurrection brewing at our borders so we need to complete the coronation ceremony forthwith, so the new emperor can take the necessary decisions to face this emergency.'

'But surely that's just a formality?' asked Ananta Varman. 'We all know that the emperor had personally chosen Kumar Kacha as his tatparigrihita heir. In fact, he called his first born the noblest of all his children.'

I could see Padmanaga's face clouding over even as Jivita kept looking at the door to see if Bhasma had walked in. 'My revered husband, the late emperor, loved all his children equally,' she said. 'He may have chosen Kacha as the heir but who knows what pressures he was succumbing to? I say we put the matter to a vote.' I saw a section of the council nodding in agreement and knew I had to nip this in the bud right then or all would be lost.

'I don't see Bhasma in the council chamber today,' I said. 'Should he not plead his own case? As far as I know, he's capable of speaking his mind.'

'*Sadhu, sadhu* ... Well said, Kumar Kacha,' chorused Ananta Varman and the ten generals seated around him.

'But why is my brother not here?' asked Jivita, his voice ice-cold with venom. 'When he left last evening, he told me he was going to the Chakrapani Vishnu temple with *you*. So maybe you can tell the council where he is, brother?'

'Bhasma and I did ride out together but we were attacked on our way there by the perfidious Nagas,' I replied, keeping my voice nonchalantly calm. 'We were not armed so we had to run for cover and I lost him in the melee.'

'My kinsmen would never do something like that,' spat out Padmanaga.

'Madam, we gave them fight even though we were unarmed,' I said. 'Would you like me to order a body search of every Naga present in the capital so we can identify the attackers? Would that be proof enough?'

Padmanaga was shaking with rage and about to shout out her reply when Jivita restrained her. 'Mother, let me speak,' he said. 'Kumar Kacha, how did you know the attackers were Naga? Were they wearing the serpent emblem on their breastplates or carrying pennants announcing their identity?'

I saw Brahma Deva shifting uncomfortably in his chair, and knew I had to tackle this one carefully. 'They wore no identification but their hissing war cries gave them away,' I said. 'Perhaps Bhasma recognized them too. They did not attack him and he simply rode away untouched.'

'I think you are holding my son prisoner because you know his claim to the throne is as valid as yours,' hissed Padmanaga. 'And now you're telling us this cock-and-bull story to explain his absence. You seriously expect us to believe this?'

'Believe what you will, Madam,' I replied, coolly. 'But think hard before you hurl allegations at the emperor elect.'

'Kumar Kacha's behaviour and bearings have always been nothing if not exemplary,' dittoed Brahma Deva. 'These accusations are unfair and unacceptable.'

'Hear, hear,' chorused the house.

I could see Jivita glare at his mother. They were on the back foot, thanks to her outburst. He waited for the hubbub to die down before speaking, 'I don't see Harisena in the council chamber this morning,' Jivita said. 'Where is he?'

'We are not here to discuss Harisena's claim to the throne surely,' asked Narasimha, eliciting cackles from the house.

'My brother has often had to fend off attacks from Harisena and his men,' persisted Jivita. 'I simply want to know where he is. Is it not possible that he's holding my brother prisoner somewhere?'

This one was far easier to answer. 'I sent Harisena to the borders on a fact-finding mission once we heard the Nagas were preparing a strike,' I said. 'He left last evening.'

'And was the council aware of this sudden decision?' asked Jivita.

'Kumar Kacha informed me,' said Brahma Deva. 'And the generals, of course. I have since shared the information with a few members of the Council of Elders,' he said.

'Why all the secrecy?' asked Padmanaga. 'Why wasn't the information shared in the house?'

'Because I didn't want to wait till today to find out more about the Naga rebellion,' I said. 'They may be your kinsmen, Madam, but if they are rebelling against the crown, they are our enemies.'

'Of course,' chorused the house.

Brahma Deva raised his hand to shush the din. 'I think we have wasted enough time discussing irrelevant probabilities,' he said. 'His Majesty the emperor had intended Kumar Kacha to be his heir, so the sooner we anoint and crown him, the better for the realm.'

'*Sadhu, sadhu*,' chorused the house.

Padmanaga stood up with a face like thunder and walked out of the council chamber. Jivita remained seated but did not open his mouth for the rest of the meeting. The royal priest, who was waiting just outside the chamber under mother's orders, came in and anointed me with Ganga water and flowers.

Soon after, we had the havan puja that marked my transition from a prince to a king. The entire council threw vermillion, turmeric and rice as Datta and I walked up to the Aryapatta throne on a carpet of flower petals. The priest used the havan ash to mark my forehead and hers, blessed us with sacred Ganga water, and placed the crown on my head.

I, Lichchavidauhitra Kacha, was now Parambhattaraka Maharaja Adhiraja. But my battle had just begun.

4
Venom in the Veins

THE ROAR RANG IN my ears and my eyes were full of blue. The sun-kissed water sprayed salt and foam on my face. I was riding the wind, and I was ruling the waves. Tantalizing and tempestuous, an exquisite expanse spread out before me. A rainbow of colours, all blue – inky blue, sky blue, blue green, aqua marine, grey blue … Crowned by the white surf, the waves swept me up on and on. I knew not where. I knew not why. Perhaps the where and why didn't matter after all. What did matter was what I saw all around – infinity, stretching from horizon to heaven. Limitless in its promise, relentless in its call, primeval, powerful, pure.

I opened my eyes but for a while I remained on the edge of my dream, still tasting the salt on my tongue, still smelling the fish-and-seaweed tang of the ocean. The dream had stayed with me ever since I first glimpsed the blue waters. Harisena and I had spent three years travelling before I became the tatparigrihita heir. Mother wasn't very keen, but father encouraged me to see the rest of our land. 'You need to know what you are fighting for,' he had said. 'Go forth and see these blessed places, son. Some day, I hope, you will bring all of it under our Garuda Dhwaja. And take our name right down to the ocean.'

My journeys took me all over Jamvudweep – Bahlik desh to Mahakantar, Kosala to Pishtapura, Kottura to Kanchi. But it was in Kanchi that I first saw the waves. Perfectly choreographed in their sweeping rush, they tumbled at my feet, washing away my foothold in the sand. I found a conch shell half-buried on the beach and Harisena showed me how to hold it to my ear and hear the roar of the waves trapped inside. We stayed at that little seaside village longer than we had first intended. The fisher folk who lived there were simple and warm-hearted. They offered us shelter in their flimsy bamboo-frame coconut thatch huts, fed us their fiery tamarind-laced curries and taught us their language. Harisena quickly tired of our travels and wanted to return to Pataliputra. But I lingered on, curiously at home among these strangers. We would have stayed much longer had it not been for a drunken braggart in our group. One of Harisena's men made the mistake of boasting that our simple merchant train was actually a disguise. We were travelling incognito, deep inside Pallava country without diplomatic clearance, and I had no desire to risk a skirmish and a ransom. So we hurriedly made good our escape, hugging the east coast as far back as Devarashtra before turning back westwards to Magadh.

Long after we returned, the memory of the ocean stayed with me. I would often hold the conch shell to my ear and hear its call. In time it grew into an obsession, something neither Harisena nor Datta could understand. When I first told her about the sea and how my dream was to go back to Kanchi some day, Datta started crying. 'You will inherit a noble and great empire; why do you need to go forth and conquer lands no one has even heard of?' she asked.

I hugged her and teased, 'You wouldn't be so afraid if you had more faith in my sword arm.'

'I know you are brave enough,' she replied unsmilingly. 'But I am not. You go away and leave mother and I in a limbo of hope and fear. You'll never understand what a bone-crunching, breath-gasping weight it can be – the weight of the wait.'

'Some day you will be the Patta Mahadevi Queen Empress,' I chided her. 'You have to be my strength, not my weakness.'

She kept quiet, but it was a grudging truce. Later when I spoke to Harisena, I realized Datta had been discussing my ocean obsession with my best friend. 'Once you are emperor, you will need to stabilize your borders and crush any enemies lurking in your backyard,' he said. 'With the Nagas on one side and Byagra on the other, you will have plenty of action on the battlefield. Distant lands like Kanchi are best left to themselves. At the most, you can send a diplomatic mission there and establish some kind of official contact with the Pallavas. That's all.'

I shook my head. 'That's not what father said. He told me to go forth and take our Garuda Dwaja right down to the ocean front.'

Harisena smiled. 'He may have meant that metaphorically. You cannot rule a land that is so many thousands of kos away from Magadh. And what's the point of waging war if not for land?'

It was a dampener, but I had to agree there was logic in what Harisena was saying. It didn't make sense to risk men and resources to attack a kingdom so far away, one that would be impossible to hold on to. So I dropped my plans of a southern digvijay and concentrated on learning how to control the court and keep enemies nearby at bay.

Except the dream of the ocean kept coming back. Primeval, powerful, pure. I would wake up with a tangy taste on my tongue, the smell of seaweed in my nostrils and promise myself ... someday, someday.

Bhasma returned to court the day after my coronation. Wild-eyed, his hair matted with dust and his uttaria scarf torn and bloodied, he stormed into the council chamber demanding an audience. I was expecting quite the spectacle from him, so was prepared. While the Council of Twelve Elders demurred, wondering how to handle a prince of the blood who was hell bent on a public showdown, I reacted immediately.

'Bhasma is my blood brother and a prince of this royal house,' I announced. 'He deserves to be heard.'

Bhasma smirked. 'I doubt if you'll feel quite so magnanimous once you've heard what I have to say,' he thundered.

'Very well, speak then,' I replied calmly, reining in my sudden desire to thrash him with my spear-butt. Bhasma was behaving like a brat as he always did when things didn't go his way. But this wasn't a weapons-training class and father wasn't around to tick him off for crossing the line. So I gritted my teeth and prepared myself for his tirade.

'My lords,' began Bhasma, 'I have come to contest the coronation of my half-brother, Kacha, because he has usurped the throne through trickery.' A wave of murmurs went through the hall as the Elders let this audacious claim sink in. Bhasma waited a few moments for effect, and then continued. 'I was attacked and imprisoned by Kacha's right-hand man, Harisena. He held me prisoner so I could not come here yesterday to stake my claim to the throne. His men only let me go this morning, knowing that the coronation ceremony would long be over.'

The hall now erupted in a chaotic din of confused voices. Brahma Deva raised his hand to silence the commotion and spoke to Bhasma, 'Your highness, these are serious allegations. You must remember, you are calling your emperor and blood brother a liar and a usurper. Do you have any proof of your claim?'

Bhasma's veneer of composure shattered, and his words gushed out in a hysterical torrent. 'Proof? You ask me for proof, you old he-goat? Can you not see the condition I am in? Filthy and bloodied, unwashed, hungry and weaponless? Does this look like a disguise to you? Who do you think would have dared to molest me, a prince of the blood? Harisena is a puppet on a string, but that string is being pulled by none other than my noble half-brother. It was entirely his plan to ask me to accompany him to the Chakrapani temple, to disguise his men as Datta's ladies-in-waiting, to organize an ambush so I could be kidnapped and held till the coronation ceremony was over and done with. You think I am a fool? You think I don't understand these games? Kacha has always been jealous of me because father made it very clear that I was as much his favourite as his first-born. My sword arm is no less than his. My mother's lineage no less than his and my claim to the throne no less than his. So why was I not given a chance to stake my right? Kacha knows this is legitimate and he is scared. Hence, the elaborate ambush and kidnapping. I demand that the council rescind the coronation and have an open debate on who is more deserving of the Aryapatta throne. I demand the council summon Harisena so he can be interrogated. Once he starts singing, my dear brother won't know where to hide his face.'

And he continued – eyes wild, face flushed with anger, forehead glistening with sweat, mouth frothing – piling insult after hideous insult on mother, Harisena and I. The council listened on in horror. I stole a glance at Brahma Deva and saw him staring in stupefied silence. It was the most dreadful scene and at that moment I decided it had to end. Right away.

I raised my hand and the hall fell silent. Even Bhasma's gibbering faded away and the frenetic whispering suddenly stopped. 'My brother is levelling some very serious allegations against me, and I feel it is my duty as the newly anointed monarch to clear these doubts before I begin the more serious work of ruling this realm,' I said, keeping my voice as calm as I possibly could.

I continued, 'Bhasma's claims are so fantastic that had father been with us today he would have laughed at them. He says he was kidnapped and imprisoned by Harisena but as this council knows, Harisena has been dispatched to the border on a secret reconnaissance mission. General

Ananta Varman will vouch for that. Unless Harisena knows witch craft, I cannot see how he can be in two places at the same time.'

I saw some murmurs and a smile or two among the faces in the council chamber. Bhasma had gone unusually white, his long face looking almost bloodless in the half-light of the dimly lit cavernous council chamber. He licked his lips in nervousness and I continued.

'As for the attack, I have already informed this house there was one. But it was not my men who ambushed us. It was the treacherous Nagas. I was unarmed and we were only accompanied by Datta's ladies-in-waiting so I had to make good our escape. I didn't realize they would kidnap their own kinsman. But then again, a prince of the blood brings in a good ransom, so maybe that's why?'

I waited a moment to take in the effect of my own words. Then I carried on. 'You may well ask how it is that I know our attackers were Nagas. No, they weren't wearing their clan colours. But their hissing battle cry gave them away. I heard it. Datta heard it. I am sure Bhasma heard it too, though he may not want to remember such minor details. If I remember correctly, the attack happened at the base of the hillock on which the temple stands. Bhasma says he was imprisoned but if you ask the temple priests they will say there was an attack and they saw some women and a few riders flee. If my men were indeed accompanying us, there would be a fight, would there not? There would surely be bodies? Some mangled horse and human flesh as evidence of the attack? But as this council knows, when it sent a search party looking for Prince Bhasma, they found no such evidence. Queer, is it not?'

I saw the elders nodding in agreement and looking at each other for affirmation, and I secretly thanked my mother for sending her men across to clear up the evidence the night I returned to the palace. She'd have known that there would be a search party, and the dead bodies bore enough weapon marks to show there had been an even fight. I found out the next morning when she came in to tell me the ambush area had been cleaned up. Without that quick action, I would have been in trouble today.

I paused for a few moments and began again. 'My lords, I was chosen by my noble father before this august chamber, as his tatparigrihita heir. I have assumed my responsibilities knowing that is what he would want me to do. I am being unjustly accused by a member of my family, even as the Nagas are attempting to form a confederacy to attack our borders. As we speak, our spies bring news that Naga kings, Achyuta of Ahichhatra, Nagasena of Padmavati and Ganapati Naga of Mathura are forming a confederacy to attack our borders and destabilize this realm. Their kinsmen and allies like Nagadatta, Chandravarman, Balavarman, Rudradeva and Matila are offering moral and tactical support. This, in effect, means most of Aryavarta is rising in rebellion against us. We need to act quickly and decisively right now. Not waste time on the wild ramblings of a jealous prince.'

Suddenly, everyone started speaking all at once and the council chamber nearly drowned in the resultant hubbub. I could catch snatches of the reactions: 'His Majesty is right', 'The Nagas need to be taught a lesson', 'Prince Bhasma is being unreasonable', 'We need a united front, not a divided house right now', 'His late majesty had chosen Prince

Kacha years ago', 'Prince Kacha is the rightful heir and has always been'. This was when the weight lifted off my chest. Bhasma had lost his last gambit. All I needed to do now was isolate him from his Naga benefactors in court. And that, given the current political situation, was not going to be difficult at all.

I raised my hand once again and the voices died out. 'I hope I have cleared this misunderstanding. But my brother is right. He is a prince of the blood and I cannot allow his manhandling to go unpunished. Given that they are plotting a rebellion right now, and attacked and kidnapped a prince of this noble house, I propose we banish all Naga representatives from the court and the capital with immediate effect.'

The announcement was met with a chorus of *'sadhu, sadhu'* as the council showed its near-unanimous agreement. I looked at Bhasma and saw his pallid face harden. He may not be as clever as Jivita but even he realized he'd lost this round. His hysterical outburst had not only cost him his chance at staking his claim to the throne but it also offered me the golden opportunity to banish his patrons and isolate him. He sat there staring, unblinkingly into my eyes, and I saw such venom there that for a moment I was taken aback. This was no sibling rivalry, I suddenly realized. There was something else here, something more insidious, a poison running in his veins. Bhasma was the enemy within, while the Nagas were the enemy without. To vanquish one, I needed to vanquish the other; sooner or later.

Two days later, the council passed the war resolution. The cavernous council chamber – its carved pillars and frescoed walls depicting scenes from the Mahabharata and lit up with 500 silver lamps – was chock-a-block that evening. The entire council was in attendance, including the Twelve Elders, the twenty-five generals, the entire royal family as well as fifty select governors from the outlying provinces. Bhasma was there too, looking like death itself, flanked by his mother and brother. The Naga contingent was absent of course – Ananta Varman had wasted no time in carrying out my orders of banishing them from court and the capital. I had also received word that morning from our spy network that the Naga grouping was in an advanced stage of battle preparedness. I needed to mobilize my troops immediately but I needed to put a regent in place first to run the kingdom while I was away.

The night before, mother, Datta and I had a long conversation and we decided that Brahma Deva was the best man for the job. I would have preferred Harisena but he was too young. Besides, I needed him next to me on the battlefield. Mother suggested I take Bhasma along with me for good measure. 'What?' I exclaimed. 'Take the snake to a snake pit – that's madness!'

'Actually it's a masterstroke,' said Datta, surprising me with how quickly and intuitively she figured out the way mother's mind worked. 'If he's with you, he can't foment trouble in court.'

'Exactly,' smiled mother, casting an appreciative look at Datta. 'Also this way Jivita and Padma will not dare hatch any schemes to destabilize the regime. Bhasma will protect you from intrigues within your own family.'

I was not terribly eager to take a disloyal and hostile sibling along with me to the battlefield but I had to agree that there was merit in the plan. 'All I need to do is bully him into coming with me,' I said with a quiet chuckle. 'That shouldn't be too tough.'

'He won't go without a fight,' said mother. 'You have to force his hand.'

As it turns out, she was right. I looked around the council chamber and rehearsed the speech in my head. It had to come out right, with just the correct mix of determination and bravado, or Bhasma would not budge. I had to make him agree before his mother and brother could change his mind. 'Years ago, one man dared to dream an impossible dream,' I began. 'Armed with nothing more than his vision and an indomitable spirit, he forged a mighty empire and secured our neighbourhood with alliances. As long as he lived, our allies stuck to the letter and spirit of diplomacy but with him now gone, they are baying for blood. The Nagas were never our friends but they were our kinsmen and allies. Now, it seems, they think of us as their enemies. Harisena has sent word that confirms what our network of spies had earlier come to us with: the Nagas are grouping against the empire. I need to march against them immediately to crush this evil intent once and for all. I urge you to pass the war resolution with immediate effect so that we can stamp them out before the enemy has had time to prepare.'

I stopped, waiting to catch my breath and get an idea of how well my speech went down with the audience. I was greeted with a moment's silence and then a thunderous applause. It took some time to die down but when it did,

Brahma Deva stepped up and asked the question everyone wanted answered. 'Your Majesty,' he said. 'Who will conduct the day-to-day business of governance while you are away?'

'I have thought of that,' I replied. 'And I can think of no one better qualified for the job than you, arya.'

'*Sadhu, sadhu* ... well said, Majesty,' came a chorus of voices.

'There is another small matter,' I continued. 'I would like to take my brother Bhasma with me on this expedition. There has been some misunderstanding between us and I believe there's no better way to re-build our camaraderie than by fighting shoulder-to-shoulder at the front. What say you, brother?'

The suggestion took everyone by surprise, but Padma was the first to react. 'My son cannot go with you,' she said. 'I am unwell and need him here beside me. With my husband gone, I need my sons to be around me in such trying times.'

Smart woman, I thought. She knows what this is about and has no desire to allow her son to become a hostage. Also, she's scared of what might befall him on the battlefield, whether by design or otherwise. 'I understand and appreciate your sentiments, Madam,' I said. 'But this is war. We, princes of the blood, need to secure our borders or there will be no legacy left for us. The Nagas may be your kinsmen but they are now our enemies.'

Brahma Deva took the cue and stepped up. 'If Prince Bhasma does not agree to go with His Majesty, that will make him a traitor for siding with the enemy. I suggest you let him go, Your Highness.'

'You'll still have your younger son here to look after you,' piped up Lichchavi councilman, Narasimha.

Padma's eyes flashed fire. 'I don't need a lecture on loyalty from the Lichchavis,' she hissed. 'My son is being taken hostage so he can be disposed of in the battlefield.'

'I give you my word, Madam, Bhasma will return to Pataliputra unharmed,' I said. 'Unless, of course, he attempts to do something thoughtless. Like running away to join his Naga kinsmen.'

'My brother will never do that,' Jivita spoke through gritted teeth.

'In that case, it is settled,' I replied. 'We march out in a week.'

5

March to Mathura

DESPITE THE ANNOUNCEMENT IN open court and full support of the entire council, we didn't actually march out in a week. Nor did I intend to, of course. I knew the capital was still crawling with Naga spies and I wanted to send out a strong intent to attack, one that would create some degree of panic in the confederacy. But our real weapon would have to be stealth, and marching out in a blaze of military glory was simply not a part of the plan. I wanted the enemy to expect an attack and still take them by surprise.

Besides, I was waiting for Harisena to return and I had made it clear to Brahma Deva that I would decide on our next course of action only after getting adequate information about the Naga battle plans. The intervening weeks proved extremely useful. Brahma Deva and I sent out our own spies on secret missions to neighbouring kingdoms to suss out which way they were likely to bend once war broke out. In public, all of them, Byagra included, seemed pliable enough. But my intelligence network brought some interesting news – the Tiger King had secretly been in touch earlier with Bhasma and Jivita when father fell ill, and the coronation drama had been a bit of a bolt from the blue.

My Lichchavi kinsmen privately reiterated their complete support to both mother as well as I. This was something to be thankful for as I needed them to secure the capital for me while I was away on the Naga mission.

The wait took Bhasma and Jivita by surprise. They'd expected me to march out immediately as announced and had, without a shred of doubt, sent word to their kinsmen accordingly. But with the Naga contingent banished from the capital and emergency security in place, entering and leaving Pataliputra had become extremely difficult. The city's gigantic iron-spiked wooden gates now remained shut at all times, and entry and exit was controlled through a small side gate that was heavily manned by imperial guards and allowed only by a signed permission from the city magistrate, Nagar Uparik Devdutt.

Three weeks later, Harisena returned, laden with information. 'The confederacy is expecting you to attack Mathura first because it is the biggest and most loot worthy city under Naga control,' he said. 'Because of this, they have heavily fortified the city and are concentrating most of their troops there.'

'In that case, we must attack elsewhere,' I replied.

'What do you mean, Majesty?' asked Ananta Varman, the only general included in our mid-night war council.

'Numbers don't win battles,' I said. 'We have to use stealth and surprise to rout our enemies. And the best way to do that is to be at two places at once.'

Harisena, catching the drift of my plan, smiled. 'I think I know what you have in mind,' he said.

'It's simple, really,' I replied. 'The Nagas expect us to attack Mathura. That's not very far from Pataliputra. And it's rich – its loot enough to bedazzle most invaders. But we are not looking for loot, are we? We're looking to prove a point. So we will attack Ahichhatra instead. It's not that heavily fortified and has a smaller garrison defending it. Which makes it more accessible.'

'You mean we will send war ships? That's the easiest route – up the Ganga,' said Ananta Varman, his eyes shining.

'More like shabby merchant vessels carrying a small, handpicked contingent of infantrymen and archers,' I replied.

Ananta Varman's smile widened. 'We attack them. They are taken by surprise. We take the city. They then ask for reinforcements from Mathura. And then you attack Mathura. Am I correct?'

I laughed. 'It's as if you've read my mind. We must divide ourselves into two small divisions, no more than 3000 men in all. The first will attack Ahichhatra. The second will attack Mathura. You, Ananta Varman, will lead the first and I will lead the second,' I said.

'It's brilliant,' said Harisena.

'It will work only if we can leave the capital in complete secrecy. Ananta Varman, you will choose your men and sail away in the dead of night. Don't sail together. Stagger the flotilla into groups of two or three boats. Under no circumstances should you attract any attention. Disguise your men but pick the best. Everything depends on the first attack going as per plan,' I said.

'Of course, Majesty,' replied Ananta Varman. 'I will get to work immediately.'

'But what about Prince Bhasma?' asked Harisena.

'I will take him with me,' I said. 'We will leave a week after Ananta Varman and his men. We too will do so quietly but we will travel by land.'

'It is far more difficult to travel incognito by road,' said Ananta Varman. 'The cloud of dust raised by a cavalry contingent is a dead giveaway.'

'True,' I said. 'That's why we will travel by night. The men will wear green shawls over their ochre uniforms to blend in with the foliage. We will carry no pennants. The foraging party will be dressed like itinerant tradesmen. There will be no scorched earth policy. We do not inconvenience common folk. The entire platoon does not move at once. We will break up into smaller units of 100 or 200 men, and stagger our move. We will eat dry food like crisp rice and jaggery so there are no cooking fires. We will stay away from the main roads and ride on the grass to muffle the sounds and leave no footprints. Remember, we must be nimble and avoid detection. At all cost.'

Brahma Deva, who had remained silent all through this discussion, finally spoke. 'There's just one thing – have you considered the fact that Prince Jivita will send word to the Naga camp the moment his brother leaves with you, no matter how secretly?'

'Of course,' I replied. 'That's why you must put my stepmother and half-brother under house arrest the moment I leave the capital.'

Brahma Deva nodded. 'It is a good plan, Majesty,' he said. 'But you are the all-powerful Param Bhattaraka Maharajadhiraj. You can use a sledgehammer to crush these Nagas. Why not show them the might of the empire? Show them what it means to cross swords with the valiant Guptas?'

I smiled. 'I will,' I said. 'When I go on a digvijay.'

The pale moon cast a gentle glow upon the curiously flat landscape on both sides of the dusty road. The summer harvest was over and the croplands on both sides looked bare, veiled by a thin mist that hung over them. This was the empire's food bowl; the silt-rich soil grew everything from paddy to wheat, maize to sugarcane. Neatly laid out, the square or oblong blocks of farmland were punctuated by clumps of mud-and-thatch huts, and neem and peepal trees here and there. Far away, I caught the glimmer of the moonlight on a village pond, its edges fringed by tall palm trees. The night air was fragrant with the smell of Mohua flowers and wood fire, the stillness of the night alive with the sound of buzzing crickets, croaking frogs, hooting owls and the occasional long-drawn baying of jackals.

The sal, arjun and banyan trees that lined our way looked like ghostly sentinels, dark shapes swaying gently in the late autumn breeze. It was late November and the Agrayan nip was already in the air. It sent an occasional shiver down my spine, though more from nervous excitement than cold.

Like every member of the platoon, I was wrapped in a thick woolen shawl that covered not only my leather breastplate but also the weapons I carried – the longbow strapped to my back, the Asi and the Khadaga broad sword dangling from my cummerbund. We rode in silence – the horses had their shoes bandaged with thin strips of linen to muffle the sound of their hoofs. Only the scouting party riding ahead carried a torch or two.

It had been nearly ten days since we marched out of Pataliputra. The infantry divisions were ferried down the river beyond the borders of Magadh and joined the cavalry upstream in small groups of not more than sixty to eighty men. We marched by night, mostly after moonrise, and not as fast as I would have liked, but stealthily enough.

I stole a glance at Bhasma riding next to me, his long jaw and hawk-nose profile set in stony, sullen silence. He did not like the idea of marching out at night, and the secrecy had robbed him of the opportunity to show to the people just how magnificent he looked in full regalia. 'Are we going on a military campaign or a cattle raid?' he'd asked snarkily when finally informed of our plans. 'If Kacha is as confident of his sword arm as he says he is, why keep everything hush-hush?'

He'd tried his best to get some answers while on the ride, routinely chatting up some of the men marching alongside him, but since no one in the contingent, except one man, Harisena, knew the entire battle plan, my half-brother was still none the wiser. Harisena and Bhasma kept their distance. Neither had forgotten the Naga ambush near the temple, and both decided it was better not to risk a faceoff in the hurly-burly of a campaign march.

It seemed to me Bhasma was not the only one upset by the clandestine nature of our campaign. Datta had been just as bewildered and worried at the thought and idea of us sneaking out of the capital, not like heroes marching out for battle glory but like cat burglars, disreputable in our disguise. I saw her tear-stained face and heard the quiet desperation in her voice every time I closed my eyes. Our last night before I left Pataliputra was both heartfelt and heartbreaking. She clung to me in sweet passion, kissing away her own fears along with my deeply buried unease. I relaxed as I always did when I was with her and felt all my unspoken apprehensions ease away. We made tender love and held on to each other after, seeking assurance that neither was able to promise. Her last words to me, however, were those of a queen, not a lover. 'Teach those Nagas a lesson they will never forget,' she said, mustering up all the courage she had in that thin, little girl body to hold her head erect. 'Come back in glory, Majesty.' As I rode away, I looked back and saw her silhouetted against a brilliantly moon-washed sky, a solitary figure standing on the farthest east-wing balcony, hugging herself and quietly trying not to cry.

Mother, though, was dry-eyed all through the short and hurried farewell, sanguine in her belief that everything would work out as planned. 'I know you better than you know yourself,' she told me. 'You never take chances. You think things through. That is why I know you won't fail. Come back victorious, my son. And keep a hawk's eye on your half-brother.'

I was jolted out of my reverie by the distant crowing of a cock. I looked up and realized the stars had begun to pale and the horizon was already turning lighter. I used my legs to spur my horse into a gallop, directing the others to follow suit. We needed to hurry and find a place to set up camp before daybreak. This flat, featureless, farmland offered very little cover. Unless we found a neatly tucked away grove of mango trees or a secluded copse of sal up ahead, we would have to disperse even more to avoid any detection.

Harisena, who was riding just behind me, took the cue and broke into a quick canter; coming up alongside me, he said, 'There's a dense thicket of sal and arjun trees just half a kos ahead. The scouts are waiting for us there. We should reach before daybreak.'

Bhasma, who caught our quick exchange, snorted, 'Another day, another hiding place. Why not smear some oil on our bodies and soot on our faces as well? To better look the part of bandits.'

Harisena was about to snap at him with an answer but didn't because of my restraining touch on his arm.

'Prince Bhasma is not accustomed to the rigours of a military campaign,' I said, silkily. 'Please make sure my brother gets uninterrupted rest when we reach camp.'

It took us another ten days of relentless marching before we reached the forest border just outside Mathura. With the early winter setting in, there was enough fog cover for us to ride hard through the nights without risking discovery, so the latter half of the journey was less tedious than when we first set out. Bhasma did not travel well. He grumbled about the lack of amenities, about not having his personal guards with him and often refused the dry food that all of us ate. 'I am a prince, I am not used to peasant food,' he would snap at the hapless camp bearers. 'Tell my brother to allow us to hunt for game at least. The tedium is killing me.'

I heard out all his complaints but remained unmoved. Allowing hunts was, of course, completely out of the question. Or, for that matter, hassling the nearby villagers for eggs and meat. We needed to travel incognito and if Bhasma wished to starve himself, that was entirely his choice. As for myself, if my men could eat jaggery and crisp rice, accompanied by the occasional ghee-soaked wheat laddoo, then so could I. The only thing that our scouts got back from neighbouring villages was fodder for the horses and pack animals and, just once in a while, a pitcher of milk.

We travelled with a very small baggage train and just ten pack mules. Apart from food and some weapons, they also carried two very important pieces of war machinery – catapults which had been dismantled into smaller pieces. This ingenious piece of equipment was Ananta Varman's idea. He'd designed it based on verbal accounts by some Buddhist monks from Kucha (modern-day Xinjiang in China). Our contingent included, apart from the soldiers and scouts, a small but efficient group of carpenters whose job it would be to put the catapults together once we reached Mathura. Catapults were more effective than battering rams as they were lighter and easier to carry but they would have certainly raised suspicion if we had carried them as fully assembled pieces. But in their dismantled form, they looked harmless enough.

We stopped at a convenient bend of the River Yamuna; it was flanked by enough forest cover to allow us to set up camp. It had been nearly three weeks since we had set out from Pataliputra and both men and beasts were sore of limb. We needed to rest, recuperate and revisit our battle plans as we waited for news from Ahichhatra and Ananta Varman.

The dense thicket where we had decided to halt was ideal for many reasons. For one, it lay at the narrowest bend in the river, even though the current here was fearsome and the eddies deadly. Still, it was narrow enough to at least attempt to ford it before we launched our surprise attack on the city.

For another, this spot would allow us a good view if the Naga reinforcements were to leave by boat instead of by land. Our spies were already keeping an eye on all the city gates but my hunch was that the contingent would prefer the river route at least part of the way because it was quicker. Besides, infantry and archers are more dispensable than horsemen, and therefore more likely to be dispatched to Ahichhatra. Allies or not, horses were expensive and sending out their cavalry would leave Mathura too weakened to resist an attack, any attack. So it was unlikely.

Ananta Varman's messenger arrived two days after we set up camp. I immediately recognized the lean and weather-beaten man who dropped to his knees to utter the royal prasasthi before me – this was Nakul, one of Ananta Varman's most trusted spies. He was accompanied by two other men, both of whom I recognized by face.

'Rise,' I said.

Nakul straightened up and produced the seal ring that confirmed what I already knew – that he was Ananta Varman's messenger. 'Speak,' I said.

'We have taken the city of Ahichhatra, Majesty,' said Nakul. 'When I left, the platoon was repairing the city's wall-and-moat defence to take on the reinforcements from Mathura.'

'Tell me how it happened,' I said. 'Don't leave anything out.'

'It took us just over a week to reach Ahichhatra,' he said. 'We staggered the flotilla and sailed in an unhurried pace so as not to arouse suspicion. Our spies had obtained false papers for some of us. The first group, around thirty strong, had no problem entering the city disguised as oil merchants. They were strip-searched of course, but they had been told to hide their weapons in their oil pitchers to avoid detection. Over the next week, we smuggled more men into the city. The plan was to attack both from inside as well as from out, and create enough confusion to allow us to storm the gates. This is exactly how it worked out.

'General Ananta Varman had planned to attack the city at dawn so as to use the thick fog hanging over the river as cover. Our boats moored a little upstream from the city gates, and the rest of the contingent simply marched forward in a staggered single file while still using the fog as cover. It was an excellent fog that morning – so thick, you could hardly see your own hands. Our main body of attackers had no difficulty reaching the city walls and climbing the ladders. It seems the Nagas were not expecting an attack, and the sentries were befuddled by the fog. Once Ananta Varman blew the conch shell, the attack began. Our boys inside set fire to as many buildings as they could to create a diversion big enough. Their soldiers then rushed to help put out the fire and in the melee, those who climbed the ladders got inside and opened the gates for the rest of us. After that it was easy. We stormed in and finished the job.'

'How long did it last?' I asked. 'And how many dead and wounded on our side?'

'The Nagas fought bravely, Majesty,' replied Nakul. 'Despite the surprise attack, they recovered quickly and fought hard. It continued for the better part of the day and it was dusk by the time we finally had the city in our control. The Nagas also managed to send word to Mathura for help. We saw the messengers leave but for some reason, the general told us not to intervene. We lost six men and as just many were wounded, some of them critically. But no more.'

I smiled. Things had gone exactly as per plan, which is something I needed to thank Ananta Varman for. His experience with topography and planning made sure that the attack did not turn into a long drawn-out siege that would not have helped us at all.

There was only one thing more to ask. 'I hope King Achyuta is unharmed?' I asked.

'Yes, Majesty. He is under house arrest. General Ananta Varman tried to parley with him but he says he is a ruling monarch and will speak to you and you alone.'

I was satisfied. 'Yes, that is reasonable. Thank you, Nakul; you have done well. Rest and refresh yourselves and your horses for you leave at first light tomorrow. I have a message for General Ananta Varman and I want it delivered as quickly as possible.'

Harisena followed me back to my tent, bristling with questions. 'If King Achyuta asked for help, how come we haven't seen the Mathura reinforcements leave?' he asked, as soon as we found ourselves alone.

That was a question bothering me too and this conversation gave me the opportunity to think things through and consider all the options. 'There are only two possible explanations,' I responded. 'Either Mathura has already sent help and we missed them somehow or they have realized this is a trap we set up and decided to wait for us to attack them here.'

Harisena took in what I said with a preoccupied look, chewing on the edges of his thin moustache abstractedly. 'If they are expecting an attack, it won't be a surprise any more, Majesty,' he said. 'They'll be waiting for us and they will outnumber us two to one.'

That was something I too was worried about. Clearly Ganapati Naga was smarter than I gave him credit for. I thought about it for a while and then said, 'Either way, we will have to risk it. We have merely 1800 men so we can't afford to lose too many. We need to plan our attack meticulously and stick to it.'

Harisena nodded. 'Our first problem is fording this bend,' he said. 'It's just too treacherous, Majesty.'

That was another thing that bothered me. Although winter meant the river was not in spate, it was still far too frisky to be crossed, particularly at night – which is what we needed to do if we wanted to avoid detection. I knew keen-eyed sentries would be watching this bend day and night from the tallest turrets in the city and an army crossing over wouldn't go unnoticed. Worse, we did not have elephants to help us cross the river and cavalry horses were notoriously temperamental beasts. They could never be depended upon not to buck and rear midstream causing both rider and animal to be pulled in and washed away by the river's treacherous eddies. It was a problem to which, for a while, I had no answers.

Finally, Harisena came up with at least a workable solution. 'Rafts,' he said, suddenly. 'We can make rafts and use them to ferry horses and men, can we not?'

'Not a bad idea,' I nodded. 'But a treacherous river can pull in a raft as much as horse and man, and we still need to make sure the rafts don't sail off course.'

Harisena was smiling. 'That can be easily done. We will wait till the fog sits nice and heavy on the river before we start. We will have men and ropes create a pathway to ford the river, and then the rafts will follow. We will move the weapons and supplies first and then move most of the men and finally the animals,' he said. 'I think I can make it work.'

I looked up and saw the gleam in my friend's eyes and knew it would surely turn out as we planned. 'Well then,' I said smiling, 'what are you waiting for?'

6

Song of the Sword

PUSHPAK SNORTED, SHAKING HIS head in impatience. My favourite stallion, dappled grey and silk-skinned, was no stranger to battle. I smoothed his long mane and murmured to him. It was a cloudless night and so bitterly cold that my fingers holding the reins were already turning blue. Every now and then, a bone-numbing wind swept over us from the river, causing the sal leaves to rustle and whisper in the dark like phantom forms, half-seen, half-imagined shadows of long-forgotten fears.

There were nearly 1800 men scattered all over the riverbank but cocooned by the fog, I felt utterly alone. The moon was up and the fog lay white and thick over the river. So thick that when I looked down, I couldn't see the ground below. The night air was full of muffled sounds – the hooting of an owl, the burbling eddies of the river, the sudden neighing of a horse and the voices of men raised barely above a whisper.

The leaves dripped dew and my woolen wrap was already sodden. The cold pierced my armour harder than any enemy sword had ever done and chilled my heart. I pitied Harisena and the men holding the ropes down in the ice-cold water to steer the rafts to the other side. This was no night to be standing waist-deep in the river.

Harisena's plan was simple. His men had felled some sal and arjun trees to hammer out makeshift rafts that were sturdy enough to carry both men and animals. A handful of our men had swum across by daylight, first to check how strong the current was, and then to string some thick ropes across the water which would come in handy when we forded the river. By nightfall, the ropes were in place and the carpenters were sewing an intricate pattern of twine and wood to create a temporary bridge. Each successive group, no bigger than twenty men, added to this flimsy pathway by laying branches and leaves along the way and making the crossover a tad less treacherous for those who came after them.

Crossing this rope bridge was no easy affair. The men couldn't use a torch for fear of burning the whole contraption down, which meant they formed a human chain and held on to the sides of this precarious rope way, feeling their way forward to the other end. Once the greater body of infantrymen had crossed over, the trickier business of carrying the horses across had to commence. For this, Harisena positioned his best swimmers along the rope bridge to help steer the rafts. Each carried no more than two horses, blindfolded and with their riders in tow, so that the animals wouldn't feel skittish mid-stream. The men used long stakes to row across, steered and helped by those already in the river. We didn't have enough rafts so each one had to go back and forth several times to carry across not only the horses but also the pack animals.

Harisena and I were the last to cross over, and by the time we were on the other side, the moon had already set. It took us close to eight hours to complete this task but apart from one pack mule and a nervous archer who had lost his footing, everyone had made it to the other side safe, but half frozen.

My first order once was to light a few fires and warm up before we started marching along the river towards the city gate. The carpenters, among the first to come across, had already started reassembling the catapults and the archers were busy sharpening their arrowheads and covering them up to protect them from getting soaked by the dew. A soggy arrow is no good to anyone, and today the archers needed to fire a veritable hail.

I remained frozen on the saddle, straining my eyes to catch a glimpse of the city's skyline in the far distance. We had more than an hour's march ahead of us and since the fog wasn't going to thin out before the second prahar gong, it gave us plenty of time to take in the lay of the land and plan our move. Bhasma stayed by my side, silently shivering on his saddle, the usual smug sneer wiped off his face. He was beginning to get an inkling of what we were planning and he didn't seem to have much to say about it. This was going to be a lose-lose situation for him anyway – if the Nagas were defeated, he'd lose his most powerful supporters in the empire. If we lost, he would find it very hard to explain why he was part of an attack against his own kinsmen.

We gave ourselves just enough time to get our bearings right before we set off again. The frontline, consisting of archers and cavalry soldiers, had already left and were expected to wait close to the city gate. Like earlier, we staggered the platoon and marched in a single file; Harisena up ahead and me bringing up the rear, with Bhasma by my side. My tiger pennant and the Garuda Dhwaja were now up, fluttering in the night wind, though we still marched mostly in the dark punctuated by as few torches as possible. We had fog cover and nothing but starlight above, yet we needed to be careful. Surprise was key. And so was stealth, till our catapults started raining fire on the sleeping city. Then we would storm in and pummel the enemy. At least that was the plan.

Unlike Ahichhatra, Mathura's defences were so watertight that our spies were unable to enter the city, despite several attempts. And those who were inside could neither leave nor send word out for fear of being discovered. Also, unlike Ahichhatra, Mathura was expecting an attack. Its boundary walls were well patrolled with archers and swords men taking turns to march up and down the rampart. Any attempt to break in was sure to be a bone-crunching nasty business. My primary concern was not to lose too many men while trying to breach the boundaries. The catapults would hurl fiery balls into the city causing a diversion big enough for the ladders to go up and our men to scale the walls. If we didn't hurry, the enemy would pour boiling oil or hurl boulders down at us. I needed this battle to be quick and decisive, otherwise we didn't stand a chance.

I had discussed the battle plan in detail with Harisena just before we set out but we both knew no attack ever goes exactly according to plan. In the hurly-burly of a charge, men behave irrationally and even the best-laid plans can go awry. That's why big armies often end up losing – it's impossible to coordinate the movements of 50,000 men. My 1800 were seasoned fighters; cool-headed and battle-hardened. They would follow instructions as much as possible. That and morale were my biggest advantages – Ahichhatra was down and my men were baying for battle glory and loot. If we kept our cool, this would be our greatest victory yet. I looked up at the sky, intending to offer a small prayer to Chakrapani Vishnu. But it was Datta's face that I saw in my mind's eye – wide set eyes, brimming with tears, even as that small nervous mouth forced itself to smile. My plucky little tailor bird I called her, tiny and unremarkable till you caught a glimpse of her magnificent heart. She will build her nest no matter what, tail up and twittering away all her fears of tomorrow.

'My brave love,' I had told her. 'Build us a nest so strong it will keep tomorrow safe for us.'

The men were wet and hungry, shivering from the drizzle that now dripped into our padded clothing and leather armour and made our teeth chatter.

'It's raining ... Can we set the fireballs alight?' asked Harisena, sounding worried. 'Without a diversion we will have a tougher time scaling the walls.'

The head carpenter chuckled. 'We have dry wood. We wrapped them well because wet wood is heavier and more difficult to plank up. You will have your fireball. Maybe not as many as planned earlier though,' he said.

'Ask your archers to start scaling the walls,' I told Harisena. 'We need some arrow cover when we breach the gate.'

'They are already on the job, Majesty,' said Harisena. 'As planned. Since we don't hear any sounds of a scuffle, I am hoping they have made it across. As have my band of guards who followed them.'

'Then it's time for the diversion,' I said. 'Fire the catapults and let's prepare for the charge.'

The rain was a dampener but seven out of the ten fireballs hit home. We heard a series of tremendous booms followed by screams and howls, and saw the flames licking the sky with delicious abandon. It was still dark but the inky black horizon was now aglow as the air filled with the smell of charred wood and flesh. In that ear-splitting din, we also heard the clear hooting of an owl. This was our secret signal that our men were in position. It was now time to push, shove and hack our way into the golden city of Mathura.

We positioned a few more fireballs, this time aiming them directly at the huge wooden city gates. 'Start hacking away at the wood, use ghee swabs and set them on fire,' screamed Harisena at those around us. This was my idea. As we hadn't carried battering rams, the next best option was to use axes to split parts of the surface of the gates, slather them with ghee and set them on fire. With the city also up in flames, the fire outside the gates, I reasoned, would not attract too much attention.

And it didn't. What did however were our men trying to force the side gate open.

I could hear a brawl of swords and spears, of men shouting themselves hoarse, of battle roars too mixed up to make any sense beyond a tremendous clangor. I heard sharp breaths and grunts, the crash of axes and the clang of swords against each other, even as arrows hissed through the air. 'They will shoot fire arrows too, Majesty,' whispered Harisena, as we stood motionless before the gate. 'My best men are inside. It won't be long.'

It wasn't. Inch by inch, the side door opened and I signalled our frontline to push through and create enough space for the cavalry charge. These were our bravest men, the spearhead of our attack, the first ones to charge into the enemy line, swinging their axes and maces around. That's how you hack your way through the enemy. It's a death trap and only the bravest or the most foolish dare attempt it. Battle after battle. Without them, a cavalry charge is impossible – the infantry always cuts a way through first.

As we pushed ourselves inside, I saw how greatly the odds were stacked against us. A greater mob was pressing down against the much smaller body of our infantrymen, bodies bumping against bodies, axes clashing, bones splitting, skulls cracking, ribs crunching, limbs ripping and bowels emptying in the great cacophony of death. Men roared and howled, vomited and whimpered. Blood spurted, brains and intestines spilled out, tongues lolled, sweat dripped and mouths frothed. The enemy was crazed with fear and they pushed forward for all they were worth. But their greater numbers were their undoing. As our men pushed back against them and the fire arrows rained down on us, those in the front tried to take cover, turning back and crushing others in their way. And so began the stampede.

Men ran helter-skelter, mangling others underfoot, focused only on the fire that rained from the sky. My men knew each other by face but the enemy, in their great multitude, couldn't tell friend from foe and in the resultant confusion, the side with the greater numbers stumbled first.

I led the initial charge, riding into this frenzied multitude, slashing our way through and spearing those our swords couldn't reach. The archers had positioned themselves on the ramparts and were now shooting non-stop, not bothering to aim since it would have been impossible to pick out targets in that melee. The charge was a furious one – it needed to be for we did not have enough men to mount too many attacks but it did the trick. Inch by painful inch, the gates swung open and then, Harisena led a swarm of his best horsemen through that narrow slit towards their bloody destiny.

This was the most frantic charge I had ever seen. Harisena and his men rode hard, straight into the enemy ranks, slashing with their swords and battleaxes in a blindingly fast dance of death. The enemy guards fell back as our frontline chopped clean through them, swinging and swerving madly, each horseman wielding more than one weapon and backed up by an archer riding pillion. At such range, the archers had a field day and they picked their targets well, letting lose volley after volley, forcing the mob to fall back, causing problems for their own cavalry that was now stuck, horse and man, in the middle of a hysterical stampede.

Whoosh, boom, sputter. The rampart guards seemed to have finally woken up, and the boiling oil and boulders were now coming down the south side to prevent any breaches from that end. They needn't have worried though. I did not have the numbers to launch a multi-pronged attack and now that we had a foot inside the door, our men were safe from being crushed under those boulders or scalded by the boiling oil. The guards could not risk targeting our men in a melee where their own compatriots swarmed all around.

I watched as this teeming mass of men – dead, wounded, bloodied, screaming, grunting, lunging, flailing, hacking, reeling – pressed against each other and willed themselves to go on. Blood lust, I thought, more potent than the most soul-stirring battle speech. Once the killing begins, bloodlust takes over. Kill or be killed, and battle strategies be damned.

I saw two of our riders go down, their horses crippled by stray arrows and the muddy ground made slippery by the earlier drizzle. The horses stumbled and as they came down in a heap, they trapped their riders below. It was a messy business. It's the worst fate that can befall a horseman – to be hauled to the ground, swarmed and hacked down by a frenzied mob. I saw Bhasma trying to ride across to help but signalled him to stop. In the battlefield, it was each man for himself. I couldn't risk more horsemen, least of all my half-brother, rushing into a situation that was already beyond help.

As our charge pushed through the melee, we finally came face to face with the enemy cavalry, already somewhat battered by the earlier stampede. The dead and wounded were now so thickly strewn at the mouth of the gate, and the muddied ground beneath us so slippery with tangled limbs, blood, faeces and mauled horse flesh that the terrain was more treacherous than the enemy waiting for us in the city square. 'Get out of here,' I shouted to Harisena. 'Push towards the city centre. We need clean, firm ground to fight. Push ahead. Hack your way through. Kill. Finish them.'

Harisena took the cue and spurred his horse ahead to ride cleanly over a group of six enemy soldiers who were crowding around in an attempt to haul him down. The horse, already maddened by the clamor of clanging swords, whinnying animals, death shrieks and battle cries, first bucked and then reared, its hind hoof hitting one of his attackers square in the face while the front hooves hit another in the chest. Both were reduced to a howling heap on the ground, and the rest scattered away so he could ride through. For myself, I had to hack and lunge my way forward, wielding both my Asi and Khadaga relentlessly to keep the enemy from crowding around. Pushpak rammed through the mob, kicking and snorting as I ran my sword into an enemy infantry man, cut down another with a mighty sweep of the Khadaga, cleanly cut open the gullet of a third and ripped open a fourth man's belly.

I saw the enemy cavalry fall back, drawing us into the bowel of the city. 'Could be a trap,' said Harisena, coming up next to me.

'We have no choice but to follow them,' I replied. 'We cannot fight here. We need to go in there and finish this. As cleanly as possible.'

'Yes, Majesty,' he said, and in a swift motion took out his battle conch shell and blew on it. He called it the

Panchajanya – named after Lord Krishna's own conch used in the battle of Kurukshetra – and it rang loud and clear, cutting through the hurly-burly of that pre-dawn scuffle. It was a signal to his horsemen to gather and attack, a fierce final charge to flush out the enemy cavalry and take over the city. It had to be now or never.

In no time, the men arranged themselves into a classic cavalry position, the chakra vyuha, with the infantry in front to bear the brunt of the initial attack. We did not have chariots or elephants, so the archers continued to ride pillion along with the horsemen, aiming their arrows at the enemy horses in an attempt to maim them and create panic in their lines. Then we would plunge in and do the real killing. 'They have elephants, sire,' shouted Harisena. 'Ask the archers to target those beasts,' I instructed. War elephants are typically given enormous amounts of liquor to make them battle-crazed. This also makes them notoriously temperamental. An elephant running amok in the enemy lines could very well do our job for us but we needed to make sure our own infantrymen didn't get trampled to death in the process.

'Jai Garuda,' shouted my men, as much to rally around our war cry as to drive home that Vishnu's mount and our patron saint was the traditional enemy of the Nagas. It was responsible, in mythical times, of nearly cleansing the world of Naga presence. The enemy infantry screeched back their battle cry, retreating deeper into the city and drawing us in with them.

I had planned a three-pronged attack with the vyuha in the middle and two smaller groups of horsemen protecting the flanks, interspersed with foot soldiers and archers.

'Aim your arrows at the elephants,' I called out. 'Target their eyes.'

My voice was drowned in a hail of arrows from the rampart and suddenly I understood why the enemy was drawing us into the heart of the city. Their archers were positioned all along the wall, which meant we had to continue our fight with a handicap, using our wood-and-leather shields to protect ourselves. But archers need time to reload and shoot, and my men knew what was expected of them. They used the tiny break in arrow shower to push ahead, keeping the entire formation as intact as possible. I signalled to Harisena on my left to branch out with one group of our horsemen, and using one of the narrow alleyways to the left to take a detour into the city centre. I did the same with the group flanking the right, leaving the main vyuha to move forward in formation, the cavalry offering cover to the archers and foot soldiers.

We galloped to the far end of that serpentine alley, and took a few seconds to take in the lay of the land. Each of the alleys led to the city centre, a large open brick-paved square fringed by the palace at one end, the elephant stables at the other and the southern edge of the rampart on the third. As I expected, Ganapati Naga had brought out his elephant corps who were standing in a neat row in front of the palace with the cavalry ranged before them. I could see one enormous elephant with a silver howdah on it and guessed that was Ganapati Naga's personal mount. From where I stood, it was at least 450 yards away, safely outside an ordinary archer's reach. What Ganapati didn't know was that I was no ordinary archer.

The square was packed with his men and horses, waiting for us to walk into what they thought was sure to be an impenetrable trap. I knew Harisena and the vyuha would wait for my cue before they charged in. All we needed was a good enough diversion; for this I needed an exceptional longbow, my own trusted weapon. I always carried it slung across my back, the quiver of arrows tucked into my cummerbund. Harisena would often complain that kings did not shoot like archers and my weapon of choice should never fall below the Asi, Khadaga and spear. But I knew how handy a long bow could be, and as I pulled that well-waxed taut string beyond my ears, the cacophony of sound and sight all around me faded away. I saw nothing but the silver howdah and heard nothing but the buzz of my bowstring as it launched the arrow through the teary morning light.

My men understood my plan the moment I aimed my shot. Within a blink, they let lose a hundred more, all targeting the elephants. Whoosh. The arrows, whirring, ripped through the morning air. We saw the volley as if in slow motion, piercing through the fast-melting morning mist as they flew through. And then, all hell broke loose.

My own arrow had hit home, burying itself in the enormous tusker's left eye. The beast, maddened by the pain, was now running amok as our second and third volleys caught some of the horses and two more elephants. The enemy cavalry, not expecting an arrow shower from such a distance, began to scatter in confusion, the horses terrified by the trumpeting elephants and the infantry trampled by them. The calm discipline from a moment ago exploded into a scene of complete chaos.

'Jai Garuda,' I shouted and rode into that deadly disarray with my horsemen in tow. 'Steer clear of the elephants. Aim your arrows at the horses. Now. Now. Now. Jai Garuda!'

My long bow was strapped back in place once again and I rode in, swinging my Asi and Khadaga. I saw Harisena spur his horse on my left and realized he was attempting to use his men to hack out a path to Ganapati Naga, now ignominiously dislodged from his elephant. I nodded and followed closely behind as we made our way through a mass of tumbling men and horses with Harisena's men forming a close ring of five around us as we rode through the melee. They used their axes and spears to clear the way, making sure we stayed away from the rampaging elephants. I took a quick look back to see our vyuha formation closing in – their orders were to take on the main body of the Naga cavalry and to make sure they did not come to their king's rescue.

When we came closer to where Ganapati Naga was standing, on what seemed like a public dais, I was greeted by a most unusual sight. The Naga King of Mathura stood back while a group of his guards took on Harisena's men. But fighting alongside them was a woman. Tall and lithe, she moved like the wind, her exquisite ruby and emerald encrusted ornaments glinting in the weak sunshine. She wore a single piece of clothing, a blood red silk sari draped like a dhoti at the bottom and wrapped tightly around her torso over one shoulder and under the other arm. Her hair was piled high in a top-knot on one side of her head and she wore jewelled hairpieces to keep the bun in place.

Like me, she carried a long bow, strapped to her back, and wielded a short sword and a spear with deadly accuracy. So fluid were her movements that it looked like some kind of intricate dance. But it was a deadly dance of death. Vaulting in the air, she dismembered one of our horsemen, landed lightly in front of my horse and rammed the spear butt into Pushpak's face. Pushpak reared in pain and I slid off the saddle to face my smiling assassin. 'Welcome to Mathura, Majesty,' she said. 'Aren't you very far from home?'

I looked at Ganapati Naga, who was still standing back on the dais, turbanless and surrounded by a handful of his personal bodyguards. 'What kind of king hides behind a woman?' I shouted out to him. 'You were plotting against me. Now here I am. Come and face me like a man. Your city will soon fall. Don't let your honour follow suit.'

Ganapati stepped forward and gibbered. 'I ... I ... wouldn't dream of plotting against the empire. You were misinformed, Majesty. I assure you. I am and always will be your most loyal ally and kinsman. Believe me—'

He stopped mid-sentence as his eyes fell on Bhasma standing behind me, and I saw the colour drain from Ganapati's face. There was such fear and rage in those porcine eyes and pallid jowls that if he weren't an enemy monarch, I would have speared him then and there. But one can't kill a prince of the blood without provocation. That endangers the lives of all royal-born and is considered adharma.

'Come and fight, Ganapati Naga,' I shouted. 'If you defeat me in a fair fight, I promise not to molest your city. If not, I will burn your golden Mathura to the ground.'

Before he could answer, the woman warrior stepped forward. 'I will fight as a stand-in,' she said. 'If you want to fight, fight me.'

'We don't fight women,' replied Harisena.

'Why not?' she asked. 'Are you afraid of being bested by a woman?'

'We are afraid of no one,' I said. 'But you don't look like a Naga to me so we have no quarrel with you. We don't fight on a whim.'

'You are right. I am neither Naga nor a local. But I am a guest of Mathura. And as long as I am here, it is my duty to protect my friends from enemy attack.'

'If you're so eager to lose your head, you can fight me instead,' Harisena stepped up.

'I am a princess of the blood too,' replied the woman. 'I will fight His Majesty or no one.'

'No no, Angai, you don't need to do this,' slobbered Ganapati Naga. 'If you're killed, I won't know what to say to your brother Vishnugopa. The Pallava regent is not a man to forget or forgive easily.'

'You will tell him the truth – that I died trying to save your honour which is my duty as your guest,' she replied calmly. 'Now, Majesty, shall we have a fair and final fight? If you're as good as they say you are, you have nothing to fear.'

I threw my head back and laughed. 'Well then,' I said, as I swung my Asi at her. 'Don't tell me I didn't warn you. Oh, and don't squeal if you get scratched.'

7

Angai

I LUNGED WITH AN almost half-hearted thrust, expecting a parry from my opponent. Instead, Angai walked away, dropped her sword and spear, and picked up what simply looked like a sturdy, well-oiled stick and a metal whip. I couldn't believe my eyes. This silly woman was going to take on the best swordsman in Jamvudeep with a whip and a staff? Both weapons looked different from what I had seen in Aryavarta before. The staff was reinforced with metal rings and had metal heads attached to its two ends. The whip was wider than the usual leather straps I'd seen and had a grip like a sword hilt, in effect making it look not unlike a narrow but fluid sword. She swung them around in a series of meditated movements and then took position, standing with one leg bent at the knee, the other straight out at an angle. Her body curved towards the bent knee, the whip hand raised above her head while she held the staff in front, almost as if she was offering it to me.

I stepped back in amazement. 'And what do you think you're doing, madam?' I asked. 'I thought you wanted to fight.'

'I do want to fight,' she replied, calmly.

'This looks more like a war dance to me,' I said. 'I am not interested in a public display.'

Angai's plump lips stretched in a mirthless smile. 'This is Silambam, an ancient martial arts form. Where I come from, this is how we fight.'

'And I suppose you expect me to drop my weapons and use a staff to face you off?' I asked.

'No, Majesty,' she replied. 'Please use whatever weapon you are comfortable with.'

I looked at Harisena whose raised eyebrows told me just what was going through his head. I caught his eye and grinned. 'Try not to kill her, Majesty,' he said. 'We don't want a diplomatic incident on our hands.'

My Kshatriya code of honour forbade me from fighting an unarmed person but since the rapier-like whip blade looked sharp enough, I decided to keep my Asi and end this farce as quickly as possible. I took my stance and swung the Asi through the air, attacking her with a series of my trademark vicious thrusts – one, two, three, four, five. My biggest advantage was speed – normally my thrusts are so blinding quick that the enemy gets no time to react. In most cases, the Asi draws blood in the first new moments of a fight. Yet, I noticed, this time around my sword blade never came anywhere close to Angai's body. She remained rooted to her spot, simply swaying out of the Asi's reach in what looked like some kind of rhythmic dancing. Each one of my thrusts were expertly blocked by the staff, even as

Angai swirled the metal whip overhead in a lazy, circular movement. Surprised, I pulled back but before I could thrust again, she attacked, the metal whip cutting through the air and lashing my sword so hard that sparks flew.

I frowned. *She's clearly well trained and acrobatic,* I thought. *And I am not used to the unusual attack arc of a stick or a metal whip. I need to focus. This won't be as easy as I thought.*

'Second thoughts?' she teased, her dark gaze piercing into mine.

'I am a warrior, not a dancer,' I replied, taking position once again with my Asi ready to thrust another series of blinding blows.

This time she attacked first – the metal whip swished through the air coming straight at my face, forcing me to block it with my sword. A second later the staff was lightly tapping me all over my body – my wrists, elbows, knees and even my toes. Each tap produced a spark of shooting pain forcing me to draw back out of reach of the staff. I realized Angai's staff was as quick as my sword arm, and she knew where to hit; at nerve points which produced the most amount of pain. I needed to neutralize that stick if I were to take on the metal whip.

As she pulled back, I unleashed a series of blows, attacking her weapon arm. She expertly blocked each one but the brute force of the strikes made her retreat to recoup. But this time, I didn't give her the chance to use her metal whip to block my aim. As she pirouetted on the spot, I swung a mighty blow at her with such savage force, hitting the staff at an angle that caused her grip to open and the bamboo stick to fall to the ground. I saw Angai purse her lips as she stepped back and swayed away from the hissing kiss of my sword blade. And then she swung her metal whip.

I saw it cutting through the air, and I suddenly knew how I could destroy her rhythm. At the last minute I crouched on the ground and raised my Asi to wrap the metal whip around its blade. The move made Angai smile; she thought she had me. She swirled around to let the whip wrap tighter and then she pulled. Except, she hadn't considered the strength of my sword arm. The more she pulled, the harder I held on, till bit by bit I could see her feet sliding through the muddy ground.

We remained locked in this position for what seemed like an eternity, and then suddenly she let go. The whiplash would have decapitated me, except I was expecting it. I twirled my Asi and flung the whip to a far corner of the field. But this move gave Angai enough time to grab her staff again. She took a new position, standing with her legs outstretched, slightly bent at the knees, body bent forward at the hip, and arms out with one hand holding the staff over her back.

'I cannot fight a stick with a sword,' I told her. 'That would be an unfair fight.'

Breathing heavily, Angai locked eyes with me and said, 'This is no ordinary stick. We call it the kampu. It can take on a sword and win.'

'Most swords, yes,' I said. 'Mine?'

She gave a slight grudging nod as sweat dripped from her forehead. 'Maybe not.'

'In that case, we call an end to this fight,' I said.

That last comment startled Ganapati Naga out of his stupor. 'Yes, yes, please, no more fighting I beg you.' He jumped, flinging himself at my feet and placing his unsheathed sword on the ground before me. 'I am surrendering my arms and my person to your Garuda protection, Majesty. Please forgive me for any transgressions or misunderstandings that may have cropped up. I promise on my ancestors you will have no more cause for complaint again. We will remain your loyal allies and kinsmen. Always.'

We stayed on in Mathura longer than I had intended. Ananta Varman joined us soon, parading King Achyuta down the main thoroughfare like a prisoner of war. Unlike Ganapati, Achyuta had too much pride and too little cunning to pretend this was anything but a public humiliation. He sat flint-eyed on a magnificent mare loaned from Ananta Varman, his lean jaw carved into a face so devoid of expression that it looked like a mask. He remained tightlipped throughout this over-the-top show of fealty to the empire, and took his leave almost immediately afterwards.

The victories in Ahichhatra and Mathura had taken the wind out of the Naga sails and the rest of the confederacy meekly submitted to the Garuda protection. They offered to increase the annual protection payment and swore never to do anything to disturb the diplomatic peace in Aryavarta. Their allies – Rudradeva, Matila, Nagadatta, Chandravarman and Balavarman – who had offered outside support to the confederacy, soon followed suit.

Once that was done, we prepared to sail back home but two problems cropped up. First, our intelligence network brought word of more trouble in Kota and I had to dispatch Ananta Varman to sort things out in that tiny western principality. This Kota problem was easily solved when Ananta Varman brought the vanquished monarch of that kingdom back with him for what turned into another round of public groveling for mercy and protection. But it did delay our departure by more than four weeks.

Then there was the second problem; that of Angai and how best to dispense with her. This proved trickier because she was both an ambassador and a woman and, unlike her gibbering host, seemed to have a spine of steel in her supple body. Worse still, she did not particularly relish leaving our fight inconclusive, and I realized that hiding behind her silk sari and glittering gems was a sword blade, sharp and unrelenting.

I met her in the palace gardens just three days after the fall of Mathura. She sought a private audience and was ushered in, be-silked and bejeweled as usual, her fierce face cast in inscrutable politeness. 'I seek a favour, Majesty,' she said, without preamble. 'Our fight the other day was inconclusive. I crave another chance to prove my mettle.'

'But you fought well, madam,' I replied. 'I cannot imagine too many warriors in Aryavarta lasting as long as you did against my sword arm.'

'But I am not from Aryavarta,' she replied.

'Where are you from then?' asked Harisena.

'From the deep south, where the wild waves wash the feet of this blessed land. Where the sky meets the sea in an expanse so blue, it fills your soul. Where the earth is red and the hills are black and the coconut trees grow straight and tall, their feet on the ground but heads high up in the heavens.'

'Kanchi,' I said simply.

Taken aback, she frowned. 'How do you know?'

I didn't answer. Instead I eyed her carefully. The king of Kanchi, as far as I knew, was a child with no siblings. 'And you must be...?'.

'Regent Vishnugopa's sister,' she replied. 'Half-sister, actually.'

I nodded. 'You're far away from home, madam.'

'As are you, Majesty,' she said.

'The Nagas are my vassals.'

'They are our friends,' she replied.

'Indeed,' I said. 'They must be very special friends for your brother to send you so far from home. A delicate diplomatic mission, perhaps?'

She remained quiet, the mask of inscrutability slipping back on her face.

'Then it is time you returned home and told your brother that this particular mission can now be safely aborted,' I went on.

'Is that an order?' she asked.

'It's a request,' I replied.

'In that case, I would prefer to stay and enjoy the beauty of this city and the hospitality of my gracious host for a few more days,' she replied. 'With your kind permission, of course, Majesty.'

'We cannot leave her behind. What if the Nagas were trying to cobble an alliance in the south as well? It's just too dangerous, Majesty,' said Harisena. He was in the middle of sending an armload of diplomatic dispatches when I walked into his work and his thoughts.

'I agree,' I said. 'We will need to coerce her into leaving. And then watch her like a hawk.'

Harisena remained silent, the feathery quill deftly held between thumb and index finger. In his hand the quill looked like a sword and worked just like one too. 'I don't like her,' he said, finally. 'Can't get a grip on her. She slips through your fingers somehow.'

I laughed. 'We're not here to tame southern princesses. But I think I know how to get her off our backs.'

When it came to instinct, I trusted Harisena as much as I trusted myself. And in this case, I agreed with him completely. The Nagas extending their influence beyond Aryavarta was not good news for the empire. This diplomatic distension meant that the Nagas were looking to find new friends to back them up if things were to go wrong. And I had no desire to allow Angai to conclude her mission, whatever it was she had come for.

The trouble was that nothing we tried seemed to work with her. Both Harisena and I had already tried gentle persuasion, veiled and not-so-veiled hints, and the occasional open threat. But Angai remained inflexible. She was Mathura's guest and unless Ganapati Naga asked her to go, she had every intention of staying for as long as she wanted. It was a stalemate.

'You've to fight this, Majesty,' said Harisena.

'Yes, I have been thinking about that,' I replied abstractedly. 'But Aryavarta first.'

'I am sorry?' said Harisena, his left brow arching into a question mark.

I realized he had completely missed my train of thought and chuckled. 'Oh yes, and her too,' I said.

'The charm offensive?'

'The joust offensive.'

'I don't follow, Majesty,' said Harisena.

'I will ask her to teach me her art ... you know ... Silambam,' I said. 'That should help break the ice. Once she starts thinking of us as friends and not invaders, she'll be more amenable to reason. You'll see.'

Harisena looked doubtful but gave in. 'If you say so, Majesty,' he replied.

I caught her on her early morning ride, racing her to the edge of the river in a brisk gallop that tasted refreshingly like freedom after the tightly coiled tension of the campaign. It was a dappled morning, the light mist giving everything around it a pearly glow. As we made our way back, riding in a slow and easy trot, I asked her about her war dance.

'It's not merely about fighting,' replied Angai. 'It's a way of life, a philosophy that permeates everything we do.'

'It's intriguing,' I conceded. 'But I am not sure how far it will get you in the hurly-burly of the battlefield. Fighting is not an art but a necessity. Killing is not pretty. It's a messy, nasty business.'

She tilted her head just a little, as if she wasn't sure how far she could allow herself to agree. Then she said, 'You think that way because you fight to overpower others. I fight to overpower myself.'

'How so?' I asked, genuinely intrigued.

'To learn Silambam, you have to condition your body and that starts with conditioning the mind. It's about channeling your prana or life blood through every nerve in your body, then using the weapons as an extension of that channel. So how you live determines how you fight.'

I shook my head. This made no sense to me, schooled as I was in the conventional art of wielding weapons to kill. To me, swordplay was neither dance nor meditation. So to hear of an art that teaches you to fight like a monk sounded intriguing indeed.

'Will you teach me?' I asked on a whim, completely forgetting my earlier intention of trying to get her to leave Mathura as early as possible.

Angai smiled. 'Maybe not, Majesty,' she said.

I frowned. How dare this woman say no to the greatest swordsman in the land? Did she even know whom she was turning down? 'And may I ask why not?' I said, my annoyance ringing through.

'You're not ready to learn yet,' she said simply.

'What do you mean?'

'I can try to teach but unless you discard your ego, you won't learn much.'

I was stunned by her audacity. *My sword arm was well-known all over Aryavarta and no one ever told me I wasn't good enough to learn. How dare this woman!*

'It seems to me, madam, that it's not my ego but yours that's in the way,' I replied. 'For all your acrobatic trickery, you still could not best me in the fight.'

'That may be,' she replied, smiling. 'Then why waste time trying to learn this "acrobatic trickery"?'

'So that the next time we fight, you can't claim handicap. I can take you down, staff and whip, as easily as I can best you in a sword fight. I don't want it to be an uneven game.'

'Fair enough,' she said. 'I will teach you all that I know. It's up to you to learn.'

We began our classes the very next day, despite howls of disapproval from Harisena. 'You don't have to do this,' he pleaded. 'We can simply tell her this is now territory under the imperial Garuda protection, and that she's not welcome anymore.'

'Expel her?' I asked. 'That won't look good.'

'I can write to her brother,' he suggested. 'Tell him to call her back. Though as the regent of a sovereign monarch, he's not obliged to listen to us…'

I smiled. 'Don't worry, I will emerge from this with my wits intact and maybe learn a new martial art in the process too. Not a bad bargain, I think!'

Harisena scowled. 'Then I will accompany you while you train. I don't trust that woman.'

I clapped my friend on the back. 'You don't trust anyone as far as I know. By all means, be there.'

The next morning, both of us reached the arena early as decided, and found Angai offering prayers to her staff and whipcord. Freshly bathed, she had flowers in her hair and had smeared her broad forehead with ash and vermillion. Emeralds and rubies glinted on her ears, arms and wrists; a red silk sari tightly draped accentuated every curve and sinew in that lithe frame. She looked like a temple priestess, I thought, a devout devadasi ready for her morning performance. Harisena and I exchanged looks, me curious, he amused. Angai caught our glance and frowned.

'Is something wrong?' she asked.

'We are not used to fighting in such finery,' joked Harisena.

'My sword doesn't make me any less a woman than yours makes you any more a man,' she replied, brusquely.

'That's a strange thing to say,' I said. 'My sword is a part of who I am as a Kshatriya.'

'And my art is a part of who I choose to be as a woman,' she said.

The next hour was spent in what seemed to me a series of meditated tumbles and somersaults. 'To understand Silambam, you have to understand the logic behind it,' said Angai. 'It is a form of martial arts first documented by Saint Agastya in his book *Kampu Sutra*.'

'Why do you fight with staff and whip?' I asked, as I re-enacted the set of calibrated movements that she was showing me.

'It's all about balance and leverage,' she replied. 'The staff and whip give you extra leverage. You back it up with deft footwork, or Kaaladi, and the hand-lock blocking technique, or Poottu. The acrobatics is only a small part of this. The more important parts are hand–eye coordination, endurance, stamina and of course, flexibility.'

'Can the staff be of any length?' I asked.

'Typically it should be three fingers from your head but there are smaller versions too which can be concealed easily,' she said. 'The Kampu staff can be reinforced or not, depending upon the use you put your craft to,' she said. 'Occasionally we also use more conventional weapons like the Vel, which is the spear, the Val, the sword and the Kedaham which is the shield.'

'When we were fighting, I saw you hit certain points of my body,' I asked, remembering the pain that shot through my veins.

Angai smiled. 'You are a sharp student indeed, Majesty,' she said. 'That's *Varma Adi Murai* or the art of attacking the nerve spots in the body. It effectively disables opponents, all but the most exceptional ones.'

I saw her spin as the stick in her hand cut through the air and lashed towards my joints. 'Watch the rhythm,' said Angai. 'In Silambam, you need to be fluid like the waves. Once you get into the rhythm, your weapons become an extension of that wave creating a deadly aura around your person.'

'Still, you fight to win,' intercepted Harisena, from his corner in the arena. 'So how is this different from conventional swordsmanship?'

'Because it does not believe that brute force alone can determine the outcome of a fight,' she replied. 'You believe in fighting hard. We believe in fighting smart.'

I shot a quick glance at Harisena and caught his eyebrow arching up in disbelief once again. *I hope all this tumbling and spinning turns out to be worth my while*, I thought. *Otherwise Harisena's eyebrows will remain permanently arched in disapproval. And I can do without that bit of facial acrobatics.*

8

Home and Heart

BY THE TIME THE Kota affair had been wrapped up, it was time for Vasant Panchami. The bitter cold of Agrayan and Poush were behind us and everything had taken on a golden hue in the limpid sunshine of imminent spring. It had been nearly three months since we left Pataliputra and everyone was now homesick. The prospect of spending Vasant Panchami's raucous revelry away from home did not appeal to most of us. Worse, Harisena's spies were bringing with them disturbing tidbits about other allies across the empire, chief among them our old friend Byagraraja or the Tiger King of Mahakantar.

'He is fortifying that bolt hole of his in Asurgarh,' said Harisena.

'What's there to fortify?' I said. 'With its lake, moat and forest cover, it's impregnable anyway.'

'Yes, but why stockpile weapons and supplies? Why recruit men? What's he up to?' Harisena wondered out loud.

Byagra had been in touch with the Nagas before but the recent downturn in their fortune should have sent a strong enough signal to all our allies, the Tiger King included. But clearly, our atavic neighbour had other ideas.

'You need to talk to Bhasma,' said Harisena, holding his temples with long, tapering fingers. A scribe's hand, I thought suddenly. But then, words could be weapons too; only sharper and less messy.

'He says nothing,' I replied. 'Except that he wants to go home.'

'Don't we all?' sighed Harisena. 'But you need to put the Naga end in order. And send that southern princess back home too.'

Harisena had a point. After his very public groveling, Ganapati Naga was proving much more intractable in private. So far, he had resolutely refused to say 'yes' to an imperial garrison to be stationed in his capital. And while the proposal for higher taxes received a verbal approval from him, he was yet to sign and seal the agreement. Instead, he was plying us with food and drink, hunts and performances, telling us to delay our departure by another week and then another and another, till he spoke to those in his confederacy. Meanwhile, my men grew fat and lazy and grumbled about the inactivity.

'I wonder what he's playing at?' asked Harisena. 'The Nagas can't do very much any more, at least not in a hurry. We have broken their backs. So why tarry?'

It then came to me in a flash. 'I know why Ganapati is trying to hold us back!' I said. 'He knows someone will attack Pataliputra while we are away. He wants them to swoop in and occupy the city knowing it will take us at least twelve days to get back.'

'Byagra?' asked Harisena, forehead creased in a frown.

'Yes. We cannot dawdle any longer. We have to return home immediately.'

'Pity,' said Harisena, his eyes twinkling. 'You won't be able to finish your training. You were doing so well too.'

I laughed. 'The princess will be disappointed,' I said.

The twinkle quickly died out. 'And what about you?' asked Harisena, his voice strangely flat. 'Will you be disappointed too?'

'You're getting better at this, Majesty,' said Angai grudgingly. 'I should never have agreed to teach you.'

I spun around, blocking her stick and swayed out of reach of her hissing metal whip.

'Don't fret,' I told her. 'This will likely be our last lesson.'

Angai stopped mid-spin and turned to face me. 'You will not force me to leave for Kanchi, will you?'

'We have no choice,' I said. 'My men and I are leaving Mathura. Since you are our responsibility, I have to make sure you are safely on your way back before we leave.'

'You are leaving?' she asked, clearly surprised.

'Yes,' I said. 'Home is calling out. Pataliputra. Mother. Datta.'

'In that order?' she asked. And then, realizing her mistake, she dropped her gaze. 'I am sorry. That was impertinent of me.'

I shrugged lightly. 'No matter. It's no secret where my priorities lie. For me, Pataliputra will always come first.'

That slight tilt of the head again, as if she half-agreed but then not quite.

'And your wife,' she asked. 'She doesn't mind?'

'Not at all. Datta knows what her role as empress demands.'

'I wish I could meet her,' said Angai, suddenly. 'I think we could become friends.'

'Datta? But she's nothing like you,' I said, remembering the fragile tear-stained smile that bid me goodbye three months ago. 'She's small and sweet. And she's no warrior. I mean she's learnt swordplay and can pick up a weapon if need be, but it's only a life skill to her. What she loves most is her nest. That's why I call her my little tailor bird.'

The severity of Angai's expression dissolved into a disarming smile, one that showed off a dimple. 'Tailor bird?'

'She builds a nest,' I said, 'with leaves and twigs. Even when the rain soaks through and the wind threatens to blow it away, she doesn't give up. No matter how scared she is, she will still hang on, tail up, sewing together a home she thinks will keep her own safe.'

'A strong woman then,' said Angai, listening rapt.

'She tries to be, I think,' I said. 'Like my mother.'

'You look up to your mother, Kumardevi?'

'My father looked up to her too,' I said. 'She's my shield. She doesn't crack easily. She can take any number of blows to protect her own. But she doesn't suffer indolence. With her, I can never be anything less than the best of me.'

For a while neither of us spoke. Then Angai said, 'You are blessed, Majesty. You have beside you two exceptional women. As for Queen Datta, I think you're mistaken. I know I have never met her, but I think in many ways she's very much like your mother.'

She trailed off and then continued. 'You see, not all strength needs to be wielded by a sword. Not all victories come with a drum roll.'

'When you are an emperor, you need the sword. And the drumroll,' I grinned.

Angai smiled. 'True. But not everything that is won by the sword can be held by the sword too. You may not understand it now, but someday you will.'

'Why not now?'

She turned her calm unblinking gaze towards my face. 'I see a lust for glory in you,' she said softly, almost to herself. 'You will plant that Garuda pennant of yours across the length and breadth of this land.'

I kept quiet, not knowing what to say to that. The spell lasted but a few moments and then Angai woke up from it. 'Pity you are in such a hurry to send me home though. Your training is far from complete even though you are a fast learner.'

I smiled. 'Someday, princess, I will come to Kanchi. You can teach me then.'

Despite our best efforts, it still took us nearly three weeks to return home to Pataliputra. In the end, I had to do some dodgy diplomacy to get around the problem of our benevolent host. When he heard that we were preparing to leave Mathura, Ganapati ambled in, forehead furrowed, hands wringing and showing every possible sign of distress. Except his calm eyes told me another tale – he was wondering what prompted the decision to pull out so soon.

'Majesty, why are you depriving me of the pleasure of your company?' he wailed. 'Have I done anything wrong? Has Mathura not lived up to its reputation as the most hospitable and friendly city in Aryavarta? Are your men not happy? If there has been any lapse on our part, please allow us to make it up to you. Do not forsake us, I beg you.'

I glanced at Harisena and saw his brow arch up. This was a clap-worthy performance, if ever there was one.

'Dear friend,' I spoke in my sweetest, most conciliatory tone. 'My men and I are honoured and pleased with the kindness that you and your city have shown us. But unfortunately, we have been away for too long now and my men wish to return home.'

Ganapati's beady eyes flicked from my face to Harisena's and then to Ananta Varman's, trying to look for signs of a trap. Then, finding no clues, he slipped back into his pretend-humility, 'But ... but ... the agreement isn't ready yet, Majesty. My scribes aren't back from Padmavati and as you know we need King Nagasena's signature too.'

I looked at Harisena and saw his eyes gleam. 'Don't worry, your Highness,' he stepped in smoothly. 'As long as we have your signature and King Achyuta's as well, we can send our own scribes to Padmavati for King Nagasena's approval. I am sure, once he sees the imperial messenger, King Nagasena will ensure the document is signed and sent back without any delay.'

'Of course, of course,' stuttered Ganapati Naga, beady eyes still doing a quick dance to look for a way out. 'But ... you see, the Naga confederation had decided that no decision about the group will be taken without the presence of at least one of the member rulers. So ... it's a matter of principle, Majesty...'

Harisena looked at me, now both brows arched questioningly. I smiled. 'I am so touched by your concern for all the little details of the treaty,' I told Ganapati. 'If the confederacy has agreed to a rule like that, of course it cannot be broken. But there's a simple solution to this. I am inviting you to come visit us in Pataliputra. You have been such a kind and generous host. Allow us to repay some of your kindness. Meanwhile, Harisena will get the document signed by King Nagasena and then you can put your seal to it.'

Ganapati was trapped. 'But, but, Majesty,' he stammered. 'Mathura needs my presence. The law and order situation is quite precarious, I beg you. The forest bandits and river pirates are such a menace. The city will need my presence to protect it.'

'Don't worry,' I said. 'I shall leave General Ananta Varman behind to keep an eye on both Mathura as well as Ahichhatra,' I said. 'Surely you agree there can be no better protector than him?'

'No better ... of course ... why not ... an honour, Majesty,' stammered Ganapati, bowing low enough for me not to be able to catch his true expressions.

I looked up and saw two pairs of laughing eyes – both Ananta Varman and Harisena had enjoyed this performance as much as I did. Ganapati Naga's theatrics were nothing if not praise-worthy. As they caught my eye, all three of us burst out, '*sadhu-sadhu*,' prompting Ganapati Naga to beat a hasty retreat to resounding applause.

Typically, if you asked one of the perennially self-absorbed, perpetually cynical *nagarik* citizens of the capital what s/he thought about Pataliputra, you would get a question in return – Purba (the east) or Apara (the west)? Purba Pataliputra, on the banks of the Ganga, was the tonier part of the city. Most of the wider streets, bigger shops, better inns and taverns were to be found here. Sitting cheek by jowl with all this coin-clinking commerce were the gleaming copper-pitcher or Kalyan Kalash-adorned homes of the rich and powerful. The imperial palace lay at the heart of this commercial and political hub.

This neatly laid-out city-within-the-city was well known for its flowers. Every home had a garden and every garden had flowering trees, vines and shrubs. The main thoroughfare leading up from the ghats of the river right up to the palace gates were lined by these private gardens on one side and a large lake on the other. In the spring, both sides would be abloom – the lake thick with lotus and water lilies and the gardens ablaze with marigold, champak, oleander, flame of the forest and, of course, the flower that gave the city its name – Patali or trumpet. So entrenched was its renown for being a veritable garden that Pataliputra's second name was Kusumpura, though the venerable Chinese monks in the city's biggest monasteries had long masticated that variant to an unrecognizable 'Ku-su-mo-pu-lo'.

For me though, the western Apara was the more interesting part of the city. Stretched out along the Sonbhadra, this part of Pataliputra grew up all higgledy-piggledy, almost without rhyme or reason. Houses jutted into each other with complete abandon. Lanes twisted and turned, split up and snaked their way between homes and hearts, and then suddenly stopped short as if they had tired of their destination. Gutters overflowed with the filth of the previous day's excess. Stray animals jostled for road and mind space, alongside buffalo carts, ox-litters and the occasional donkey or horse rider. Pedestrians, big and small, made way.

Here too there were flowers but just like the people, they grew wherever they could, unintended, untended and untamed. Not brick paved like Purba, Apara's dusty and muddy lanes would suddenly erupt in a riot of colour – the bright orange of a flame tree in summer, a carpet shower of coral jasmines in autumn and the rich red of silk cotton in spring. Here too the trumpet bloomed, a defiant splash of vivid yellow creeping wantonly out of cracks and crannies or anywhere it found just a fistful of earth to dig its roots into.

In this chaotic mix stood the Apara homes. Brick-laid, mud-plastered and often painstakingly painted with turmeric and vermillion, these humble homes made up with character what they lacked in luxury. They stood cheerfully side-by-side, white rangoli on their doorsteps, daring the chaos of the road outside to cross their thresholds. And that's what I liked about Apara – this random mass of homes and humanity buzzed with an energy and vigour that was infectious. Far away from the pristine flower-lined avenues of Purba, here throbbed the very heart of the realm. Simple mud-plastered walls came alive with weird and wonderful graffiti of gods and demons, often underlined with some ribald political humour. Tumble-down taverns with disreputable clientele were patronized by some of the best poets and artists of the day. The courtesan-dancers of this quarter were known as much for their carnal creativity as for their knowledge of the Mandakranta metre. (The joke was that you couldn't become a poet of any consequence unless you learnt your rhetoric and prosody in the arms of an Apara courtesan.) The streets pulsated with enterprise and exhaustion as people begged and bought, stole and saved, cheated and created, fought and forgave, made love and occasionally murdered each other. It was a world far away from the flowery order of Purba but it was a world that wore no masks to hide its scars.

It was Harisena who introduced me to it. He had spent his childhood on these mud-spattered streets before his father Druvabhuti gained distinction, first on the battle field and later in court, as the *maha danda nayaka* (police chief). And he never forgot where he came from. Neither did others, of course. It's not easy to cross over from Apara to Purba without raising some hackles in court hierarchy. And Harisena's father, despite his change in fortunes or perhaps because of it, had raised many.

This was one of the reasons none of my half-brothers liked Harisena very much, dismissing Druvabhuti as a parvenu and his son as a bazaar boy. In fact, when Bhasma and Jivita tried to poison father's mind against him – suggesting that Harisena was exposing me to the worst rough necks in the kingdom and initiating me into the pleasures of opium-laced Roman wine – the rest of my half-brothers heartily backed the two of them up.

Not all the allegations were untrue, of course. Whenever we found the palace air too difficult to breathe, Harisena and I would slip away, incognito, for a night of Apara revelry which ended with both of us seeking refuge at his favourite dancer Ragini's bordello. Only one man knew what we were up to – the city magistrate, Devdutt. It was important to keep him in the loop if we were to get into a scrape in Apara, but he was Druvabhuti's man through and through and could therefore be trusted.

More than our romps, what I enjoyed was the freedom that my anonymity offered during such excursions. Very few people on the streets or in the run-down public places that we went to had any connections in court. This meant, shorn of my finery, I could slip into another skin quite easily. As crown prince I did not have too many public duties and my face was therefore less likely to be recognized.

There were, of course, other reasons I found these outings interesting. For one, it gave me a good idea of what people were talking about outside the echo chamber that was the court. For another, the Akhara wrestling rings here attracted the vilest, most desperate and the bravest young men in the empire, and were Harisena's favourite hunting grounds for both foot soldiers and spies. Which is why I intended to continue these nocturnal visits even after becoming emperor, though less frequently and under more elaborate disguise perhaps.

I suggested a night out just days after our return to Pataliputra. Our spies had, so far, not come up with anything more on Byagra. And with Ganapati safely ensconced in the palace, the Naga threat was effectively under control. And yet, I felt a nagging unease in my bones. Something was not quite adding up.

'Why must you assume peace is invariably only an interlude?' asked mother, for once at variance with me.

Datta, uncharacteristically voluble, said tartly, 'He thinks it's the lull before a storm. He thinks he needs a digvijay to awe Jamvudweep into submission.'

Mother turned her keen gaze on me. 'Kacha, what folly is this? Don't look for trouble when there isn't any.'

I glanced towards Harisena who held my gaze and shook his head almost imperceptibly. He wasn't going to open his mouth and wade into what he thought was a family discussion. I wished he did though, but I also knew it would earn a sharp put down from mother. I had to do this on my own.

'Byagra is plotting something,' I said. 'My instincts tell me so. I am only gathering intelligence right now. Once I know more, I will take him on. If something has to be done, I will do it.'

'So where's the digvijay coming from?' asked mother.

I looked at Datta, knowing this tidbit of my dream shared with her must have therefore leaked from her. She quickly looked away.

'It's something I have been thinking about,' I said. I saw Harisena look up, startled. Even he had no idea about any of this.

'Kacha, you are now emperor. You don't have the luxury of daydreaming,' said mother.

'They are not day dreams,' I shot back. 'The more I think about it, the more convinced I am that the only way I can keep our so-called allies in check is through a spectacular show of might. I have to prove to them that my sword arm is something to be feared and respected. Once done, it will act as a deterrent for the entire length of my reign.'

Mother remained silent. I saw the blood drain from Datta's face while Harisena looked surprised. Finally, it was he who spoke. 'But Majesty, taking the Garuda Dhwaja across Aryavarta will leave the capital open to both invasion and insurrection. Can we afford such a risk?'

'I will not do anything to endanger Pataliputra,' I replied. 'But this campaign is now a necessity. It's no longer a question of "if". It's a question of "when".'

I lay back on familiar blue silk bolsters, now discoloured with usage, and kept an ear out for the conversation going on in the room. Harisena and I were back at Ragini's somewhat tawdry boudoir, thankfully dimly lit by a solitary lamp which meant large swathes of the room were in complete darkness. I remained motionless on the couch – smothered by Ragini's limbs entwined through mine, and the old quilt that conveniently covered both her modesty and my identity – and listened. Sitting on the ground nearby, Harisena was conducting an-almost whispered interrogation of one of his informants.

'And you say there are many of them?' he asked.

'Yes,' replied the wiry young man who sat cross-legged on the ground. 'They are all atavic tribesmen. Some are selling honey; others animal fur. Some are buying beads and cowrie shells in exchange for fishing hooks and flint arrow heads.'

Harisena remained silent for a while. Then he pressed on, 'Are they all from Maha Kantar?'

'No. They are from different atavic tribes.'

'And have they been in fights or any such things?'

'No. They keep to themselves. They do ask a lot of questions but that's not unusual among trades people.'

More silence followed. Then, Harisena once again asked, 'Are there any merchants or mendicants from anywhere else roaming the streets?'

'Only Maha Kosala. They are here to sell their famed sweet meats.'

'Is that out of the ordinary?'

'No, not really. They come every year but there are more of them than usual this time.'

'How many of them are in the capital right now?'

'I am not sure but my guess is at least eighty.'

There was silence for a minute or two following this. And then the sound of shuffling feet as the young man walked out, meaning Harisena had dismissed him.

'You can come out from under the covers now,' I heard Harisena's voice call out. 'Unless you'd rather continue.'

I threw the quilt away and got up, laughing. Ragini, still as luscious in her fourth decade as she was when we first met her, stretched like a cat, smiling at both of us. 'You boys obviously want to talk,' she drawled. 'Shall I send in some Asava rum?'

Harisena grinned at her. 'You are a complete marvel.'

'Aren't I just?' She winked, lazily draping the quilt to cover her still deliciously curvy nakedness. 'Don't worry, I will make sure you two are undisturbed.'

Harisena peeped out after she left and then softly closed the door. We sat down on the couch and looked at each other. 'Well,' he said. 'What do you think?'

'There's something afoot,' I replied. 'I was suspicious before. Now I am certain.'

'But Kosala too? Or should we dismiss that little nugget?'

'We dismiss nothing,' I replied. 'If Kosala's traders are crowding here at the same time that Byagra's men are roaming around selling honey, they are both to be suspected. And the conspiracy is far bigger than I'd thought.'

'I can send my men to both Maha Kosala and Maha Kantar,' said Harisena. 'You know ... to find out a bit more.'

I nodded. 'Yes. And maybe you can get magistrate Devdutt to arrest one of these atavic honey sellers on some trumped up charge, and try and interrogate him. See if he sings. Though as a foot soldier he may not know too much. But still it could throw up something.'

'And once we know more?' asked Harisena. 'Another battle or a digvijay?'

I smiled and clapped him on the back. 'We shall see,' I said.

9
Dreams of Digvijay

ANOTHER NIGHT, ANOTHER WAR council. I stretched out on the bolstered couch and took a deep gulp of the Roman sura wine; it's salty tang brought a sudden flash of sea blue and a glint of emeralds and rubies on a sinewy arm. I frowned and focused. Harisena was speaking.

'My intelligence network has come up with some startling information,' he said. 'It seems there has been some exchange of men and materials between Maha Kosala and Maha Kantar, and Byagra has been in close contact with his neighbour ever since His Late Majesty fell ill.'

'Is that unusual?' asked Druvabhuti. 'They are neighbours, after all. And both are atavic kingdoms.'

'It wouldn't have been unusual under normal circumstances. But these aren't, are they?' asked Harisena archly.

'This also needs to be seen in context,' I said. 'Both Byagra and Mahendra have been stockpiling arms and recruiting men. You do that when you are preparing for battle. There are no border skirmishes being reported anywhere in either Aryavarta or Dakshinapath. So what are they preparing for?'

'But Majesty,' said Brahma Deva, 'both Maha Kosala and Maha Kantar are firmly in Dakshinapath. Is it necessary to go after them?'

'It is,' I said. 'If we want them to get the message, once and for all.'

Now mother spoke up. 'You don't need a military expedition for that. You could send a diplomatic mission. Ratify the alliance your father forged. Threats and diplomacy usually work well as a deterrent. Don't rush into battle when words can work just as well.'

'Diplomacy worked well with father because he had already earned his reputation on the battle field; his adversaries knew what they were up against,' I replied, slightly annoyed with this shield of opposition that kept popping up.

'You have earned a formidable reputation after the Naga expedition, Majesty,' said Brahma Deva. 'There aren't too many people in Jamvudweep who haven't heard of that daring raid.'

'But it does not seem to have convinced any of you. So why should my fellow rulers believe that?' I replied.

'But what about Pataliputra?' said Datta, uncharacteristically candid in a war council. 'If you march out towards Dakshinapath, you leave Magadh in danger of being invaded. Even if we send word to you, it will take you months to get back. Have you thought of that?'

'I have,' I snapped back. 'I will leave Brahma Deva in charge of daily governance as before. Narasimha and his Lichchavi forces will back him up. Druvabhuti will be in charge of the imperial garrisons. I shall take half the forces and leave the rest to protect Magadh. And I will appoint Ananta Varman to be in charge of all the Naga regimes and reinforce him with more men.'

'The Nagas will not like it, Majesty,' said Druvabhuti.

'The Nagas don't matter any more. Their kingdoms are effectively part of the empire now. That treaty they signed makes them puppet vassals and they know it.'

Harisena nodded. Then he said, 'Ganapati Naga wants to go back. He has been whining about missing his family and the evening arti in Mathura.'

I chuckled. 'Then send him back. As long as Ananta Varman is stationed there, he will keep all three Naga kingdoms quiet.'

'So we start with Kosala?' asked Harisena.

'Yes, I shall take on Kosala first and then Maha Kantar, both of which are just over a week's hard ride from Pataliputra.'

'And then?' Datta persisted. 'Once you go further down? Further away from us?'

'If our expedition goes as planned, our victories in Kosala and Maha Kantar should secure my reputation,' I replied. 'That will be protection enough. Till I return.'

'Can you not do this in bits and pieces?' asked Brahma Deva. 'A southern digvijay will keep you away from Magadh for at least a year, if not longer. Is it safe, Majesty?'

'This is not just a digvijay,' I said. 'It is a strategic mission. I am sending out a message to all the sovereign rulers who have not yet bent their knee to me. Raise your arm against me and I will come and crush you – no matter how far from Magadh you may be. Accept my Garuda protection and you have nothing to fear.'

'But all of Aryavarta already bend their knee to you,' said Datta. 'Do you need Dakshinapath as well?'

'I want all of Jamvudweep,' I replied.

The intelligence from Kosala and Maha Kantar was convincing enough for Devdutt to interrogate some of the tribal tradesmen in the city. As I had suspected, they did not know much. But even those stray morsels were enough to give us an idea of what was cooking in our atavic neighbourhood. The plan had been to smuggle in enough irregulars into the capital dressed as tradesmen. Then, Byagra and Mahendra were to send in a combined force to take on Druvabhuti and the Lichchavis. It was a well-devised plan and the atavics used our three-month Naga campaign to smuggle in just under 200 men into the city. Their spies had informed them that Ganapati Naga was to keep us in Mathura till the start of the summer, so they were moving accordingly. Our sudden return upset their plans.

'This proves Ganapati's role in the conspiracy,' said Brahma Deva.

'So it does,' I replied. 'I have instructed Ananta Varman to keep him under house arrest until the atavic issue is sorted out. Meanwhile Ananta Varman can run the administration in my name till further orders.'

'The Nagas won't like this, Majesty,' said Druvabhuti.

'Neither do I. The difference is that the Nagas don't have a choice. I do. If there's even a murmur of resistance, Ananta Varman has my permission to crush it.'

Once again, I was greeted by an eloquent silence full of dissent. This constant parlay was beginning to wear me out. I looked out and saw the setting sun cast an orange glow over the river. Always mighty, the Ganga now looked magical, its waters rippling like molten gold, reflecting the palette of a dying day splashed across the sky above. Inside, the shadows grew longer, the fast fading light slowly hiding the faces of those around me. Familiar faces. Friendly faces. How well they hid what they felt on the inside.

Mother and Datta had made their apprehensions clear but the others hid behind a non-committal silence. Harisena, forever cautious with his words, was drumming rhythmically with his fingers. What was he thinking? I knew he loved a good, successful campaign as much as I did but he did not share my disdain for diplomacy. Did he share Datta's apprehensions too? Brahma Deva, ascetic and inflexible, sat ramrod straight, his white beard outlining the rest of his face that was lost in darkness. He had served father well but how far can old bones carry the weight of new ideas? Dhruvabhuti and Narasimha were completely engulfed in the shadows, just a dark smudge where a face should have been. Darkness could be so illuminating. It's only then that people drop their borrowed faces. I suddenly missed father dearly. Did he have to fight this too? This stranglehold of prudence and precedence? Did it haunt his dreams? Chain him to a life less lived? As he became more the master of the realm, did he become less the master of his own destiny?

Later that evening, I walked into my bedchamber to confront my biggest weakness. I found Datta standing by the window, a tiny frame swallowed up by the folds of her sari. She looked distant, like she was withdrawing into herself. My heart lurched when I saw her, my tiny tailorbird trying so hard to fight the storm. Then she turned around to face me and the anger in her eyes hit me like whiplash.

'I hope you are happy now,' she whispered. 'It's my fault. I expected you to put us first, just this once.'

'Us?' I asked, not quite following.

'Me and our unborn child,' she replied.

I closed my eyes and felt only regret. 'I didn't know,' I whispered.

'Would it have made any difference if you did?' she asked.

I did not reply. I couldn't tell her the truth and she'd know if I lied. The campaign was now an urgent necessity. I could not have backed away even if I wanted to. Kosala and Maha Kantar needed to be put in place. I had no choice.

'Didn't think so,' she murmured under her breath.

The silence sat between us, impenetrable; my dreams and her hopes permanently at war with one another.

Then she spoke. 'Will you go as far as Kanchi? To meet *her*?'

I looked up startled. Today was my turn for surprises.

'Harisena told me,' she said.

'Angai was a pawn in a diplomatic game,' I replied. 'Harisena should know better than to carry tales.'

She shook her head firmly, wrenching a few stray curls free from the elaborate coiffure they'd been subjected into. 'That doesn't answer my question.'

'I took lessons in a southern martial art from her. We never met in private.'

Datta gripped my arms and shook me. 'Look into my eyes and tell me that's all there is to it. Look at me, Kacha.'

I looked into her eyes and then lowered my gaze. I could not hide it from her anymore than from myself.

'I thought so,' she said quietly, and turned her face away. 'You can marry her, you know. You don't need to go on this wild goose chase all over Dakshinapath for her. Even the council will hail it as a diplomatic triumph.'

I held her by her shoulders and pulled her close. 'This is *not* about her. Datta, don't you see? I have to do this for the future. *Our* future. I shall leave behind a legacy so well knit, it will take another hundred years and a thousand adversities for the seams to come loose. It's what father expected of me!'

She buried her face in my chest. For the longest time she stayed limp in my arms. I could feel her nails digging in and her angry breath burn my skin. It felt like a lifetime before the fury dissolved into tears. They came slowly at first, quietly, imperceptibly. Then suddenly there were great heaving sobs that shook her frail body and broke my heart. Her tears bathed my uttaria scarf and washed away the anger. And she became what she always was – my frightened little tailorbird, looking for a nest in the storm. I held her in my arms and whispered into her unruly curls, 'I am sorry. I have not been the husband you expected me to be. But if you truly love me, can you not let me go? Just this once?'

I got no answer from her. But perhaps, I didn't need to.

We began preparations for the campaign almost immediately. Summer was fast approaching and I intended to complete the expedition before the rains came in. It is impossible to travel or fight in the pouring rain when the ground below turns into boggy slush and the swollen rivers become even harder to cross. Besides, both Maha Kosala – or Dakshina Kosala as it was often called – and Maha Kantar were known for their impenetrable forest cover. We had to complete our battle preparations in under three weeks and set out well before Baishak (mid-April to mid-May) set in. It would be hot, though not as unbearable as the scorching Jaistha (mid May to mid-June). Still, with all the forest treks before us, it was better to brave the heat than take on the rainy season.

Unlike our Naga campaign, I had no intention of keeping our attack covert this time round. We were going to march out in full view of the entire city – a tactic suggested by Ananta Varman when he heard of our plans. News, particularly battle news, travels fast. And nothing intimidates better than the sight of the imperial forces marching out in full regalia.

Funnily enough, Bhasma wanted to join me once again in this campaign. I was initially skeptical about his request till Brahma Deva explained his reasoning. 'The Nagas are hopping mad. They feel Bhasma has betrayed their cause by becoming a part of your campaign. He is running scared, Majesty. He fears assassination attempts if he were to stay back in the capital. Marching out with you will protect him from his own kinsmen.'

I had another strategy this time that was very different from the Naga campaign. We took with us a much larger contingent – as many as 8000 men, including 4000 horsemen and a substantial baggage train. The plan was to travel by road, so we took replacement horses, pack animals and a section of my elephant corps as well. Harisena was in charge of the archers and infantry while Bhasma and I were in charge of the cavalry and the elephant brigade. Our big problem, of course, was the terrain. Kosala was deep in forest country and though not as impregnable as Byagra's Asurgarh, it was still not easy to access. Harisena had used threats and bribes to turn a handful of atavic traders to our side. These men now helped our scouting parties and guides. Like before, we weren't carrying battering rams. Instead, we carried the dismantled catapults to help storm enemy fortifications.

Due to the great distances involved, we charted the route carefully before starting out. The road from Kosala (modern-day Raipur, Bilaspur and Sambalpur districts) to the deep South goes through Mahakantar (Kalahandi, Koraput and Bastar region) and is an east coast offshoot of the southward route that traders dubbed Dakshinapath centuries ago. Because of the forest terrain, I would have preferred to fight only with cavalry but Harisena insisted we take a large enough group of archers along with us as well. The good news was that Bhasma was in much better spirits this time around. First, the atavics were not his kinsmen so there was no conflict of interest in his mind. Second, a forest march meant plenty of game for the pot so he would not be forced to chew husked rice and jaggery with the other men.

The first week breezed through in a blur of hard riding, hunting and simply battling the unforgiving terrain.

Druvabhuti had actually encouraged the atavic traders to leave the capital once we had marched out so that they would carry exaggerated eye-witness accounts back home to their masters. Harisena added to this by recruiting a large company of itinerant bards whose job was to go from city to city, spreading the word of a mighty military campaign. 'The more people hear, the more they will fear,' he told me. 'Your job will be half complete by the time you reach Kosala.'

I knew my biggest challenge so far was the terrain. This was densely forested land and the narrow mud tracks that snaked through the impenetrable vegetation could only accommodate a single file. Which made us vulnerable to attack from both wild animals and atavic tribesmen. Not to mention the swarms of bloodsuckers at every step – snakes, leeches and scorpions on the ground and a myriad insects buzzing in the ear and crawling up our arms and legs.

I was used to jungle travel and hunts, but I had never seen forest as thick as these. All around us, tall trees grew in jumbled profusion, their canopies high above blocking out the sun even at midday. Below, the world was dark and a dappled green. Only shard-thin slivers of light made their way through the thickness of leaves above and glinted off a beehive here or an ant hill there; a snake slithered in the undergrowth and fat centipedes crawled up twisted creepers. The relentless battering of woodpeckers and every once in a while the brilliant flash of colour in a pair of butterfly wings were the only distractions. No matter how quiet it got, this primeval wilderness always buzzed with life. Both the undergrowth and the overgrowth teemed with creatures big and small. Here a troop of monkeys swinging gaily from branch to branch and there the scrunch of an antelope scurrying for cover in the dense elephant grass. Foxes followed our footsteps on the sly while rabbits and field rats scampered into their burrows. Mongoose chased green vine snakes and suddenly we stopped in our tracks to allow a deadly king cobra to slither away. Bhasma slid off his horse and offered a simple prayer and some milk to his family deity, seeking protection against snakebites. I found many of my men joining in too – fighting the Nagas on the battlefield was one thing, but taking on their serpent avatars in the middle of nowhere was quite another. None of us wanted to die of a snakebite so it was better to appease this king of snakes.

Apart from snakes, this rocky landscape was also full of scorpions, whose venom could be just as lethal. We carried big pouches of salt to sprinkle on our way and the scouts in front and behind us tapped the earth with their sticks to forewarn any creatures hiding in the grass that human feet were soiling their virgin land. After nightfall, this vast universe came alive with sounds – crickets buzzing, owls hooting and every now and then the baying of jackals. We set up camp around crackling fires and took turns to stay awake. This was both wild boar and tiger country, and I had no desire to face an unexpected attack in the middle of the night. We also steered clear of elephant herds – among the most fearsome beasts in the wild – though we heard frequent trumpeting in the distance. I had hoped to hunt big game during the march but apart from boar and stag – both of which helped liven up our meal times – we didn't have much luck. Both Harisena and Bhasma were enthusiastic hunters but I was reluctant to spend too much time in sport. Game for the pot was one thing but taking time out for serious hunts would delay our mission. This was a military campaign after all and we needed to move as quickly as possible before the weather turned hot and forest fires turned this route into a death trap.

Already it was uncomfortably hot by day. The earth seemed to emit waves of heat that simmered in the stillness of the afternoons. By midday it became unbearable. The thick dust-dry air made every pore in the body sweat and it became difficult to breathe. So we would start out early and rest during the hottest hours of the day. We would begin marching again by late afternoon and continue till sundown before setting up camp. Our scouting parties cleared the tracks as we marched through, widening the path and cleaning the undergrowth on both sides as much as possible. I did not wish to lose either men or animals to snake or scorpion bites, and we had to be careful about leeches in the water. Thankfully crocodiles weren't common in this region so we had only to look out for terrestrial animals when we approached a water hole.

Typically, I used the afternoon hours to catch up on intelligence dispatches and chalk out battle plans with Harisena, while Bhasma and his men headed out for the daily hunt. He'd return late afternoon laden with pheasants, peacocks, rabbits and occasionally wild boar raising a cheer among the kitchen staff. The forest also teemed with fruits and berries, and the foot soldiers had already started sampling some of the local fare including a fiery chutney made from red ants, scrambled ant eggs and Mahua liquor. The baggage party also scoured the forest for tangy green mangoes, sickly sweet jackfruit, local figs and the juicy

Kendu fruit, all of which we learnt to cherish during that long, sweat-dripping march.

Apart from the occasional bear and leopard attack, our party remained safe for the most part. But we did lose a few men to a strange shivering fever caused by mosquito bites. Progress was slow with 12000 soldiers and another 4000 baggage and scouting men so by the time we reached Kosala, we'd been on the road for more than two weeks. King Mahendra's capital city, Shripur (modern-day Sirpur, 40 miles north-east of Raipur), was an imposing mud brick fort on the banks of the Mahanadi River. Our first glimpse of it, coloured by the magic light of impending dusk, left us speechless. Its red walls, the deep green forest cover surrounding it and the rippling grey of the river made it look like a fresco, too perfect to be real.

It shimmered in the distance beckoning us to test our fortune. And earn our reward.

Or retribution.

10

War in the Wild

WE SPENT THE NEXT couple of days meticulously tracking the terrain. The Kosala fort faced the banks of the Mahanadi River and was surrounded by thick forest cover on three sides. An entirely mud-baked structure, the fortified city's first defence was a circular wall taller than an elephant. Beyond that was a second, slightly higher wall and so the cityscape after this dual-layered protection remained permanently hidden to the outsider at the gates.

Like fortresses in Aryavarta, this atavic fort too had sentry towers all along its outer rampart. It also had guards stationed on the second rampart to catch enemy targets stuck in the narrow gap between the first and the second boundary walls. This gap, we were told, was so narrow that no more than two people could enter those tunnels side by side, thus making them a death trap under an arrow shower. Our atavic guides also informed us that inside the fort walls, the city itself was a maze of tunnels – one of the reasons why this fort was considered virtually impregnable.

The good news was that the Mahanadi, a mighty and fearsome river during the rains, now looked tame; its flow intermittently interrupted by dried up patches of the riverbed. With our horses and elephants, it would not be difficult to cross the river, I figured. Though wide and free-flowing where the fortified city stood, the riverbed had already started to dry up a little over two kos (just over 6 kilometres) upstream so we decided to cross the river at that point.

The fort itself looked solid enough, its wooden gates on all four sides had been fitted with spikes to keep away an elephant charge. The walls looked as wide as our palaces but, Harisena pointed out, they were made of mud, not brick and stone, and so could be rammed in if sufficient force were to be used. Our scouts brought us information that the southern face of the fort, facing the thickest part of the jungle, would probably be the easiest to storm as the walls were not uniformly thick and some parts were in urgent need of repairs.

'Mahendra clearly thinks the river and the forest cover is enough protection for his people,' said Bhasma. 'His fortress isn't as stout at the back as it looks from the front.'

'That's because the atavics don't expect the plains people to attempt jungle warfare,' I said. 'Our spies have been talking to some of the guards and they are quite sanguine about that. They expect an attack from the front or the sides. Not from the back.'

'Then it's time we surprised them.' Bhasma grinned.

'But the double boundary wall could be tricky,' said Harisena.

'How do you propose to get around that problem?' asked Bhasma.

Harisena was quiet for a moment or two. Then he said, 'I have a plan. We storm the outer wall, breach it, and then stock pile firewood into the gap between the two walls.'

Bhasma brightened up. 'Then we use fire arrows to set it alight and allow the sentries on the second wall to roast or get off their posts,' he said.

I wasn't convinced. 'If the gap is alight, how do we enter?' I asked. 'And remember, the rest of the city is also a maze of tunnels. The enemy will use snipers to pick us off one by one. It won't work.'

'So what do we do?' asked Bhasma.

'We must attack from the south,' I said. 'That's where they least expect a charge.'

'We will need to cut a way through impassable jungle,' said Bhasma.

'We will attack in the classic Garuda Vyuha formation,' I said. 'The beak, comprising some of our best men, and a strong contingent of scouts will clear the way for us. The head will comprise the elephant corps. The wings – our cavalry – will spread out and attack from two ends, the eastern side to create a diversion and the southern face to create a breach.'

'But how do we breach the walls? And do we cross over with our entire force?' asked Bhasma.

'We use elephants,' I said. 'Those beasts can swing heavy iron balls to smash a hole in the wall. We will fell some trees and use them as battering rams as well. And we will do all this under a hail of fire balls from our catapult. We will keep some reserves on this bank of the river so that if need be we can call on fresh forces. It will confuse the Kosala scouts into thinking we'll cross the river and attack,' I said.

'So we take most of our elephant and cavalry corps across?' asked Harisena.

'Of course. We can use the larger islands midstream as our base. Station some of our pack animals there. It is just outside their arrow range so we should be safe.'

'And the tunnels?' asked Harisena.

'We can't neutralize the tunnels,' I said. 'So we will pay our way in.'

'Bribes?' asked Bhasma.

'Yes, we have been contacted by Mahendra's younger brother and first cousin. There is serious discord within his own family. If we bribe them well, they will help us infiltrate the tunnels. That, as far as I can see, is the only way we can overrun the place.'

Harisena's brow remained arched in a question mark. 'A man who betrays his family can also betray us,' he said.

'I agree. That's why we need to be careful while dealing with them. Give them too much and they could turn too greedy. Give them too little and they could betray our presence,' I said.

'It could work depending on what their weapon capabilities are,' said Bhasma.

'The trouble is they have elephants too,' said Harisena. 'And a tiger brigade I am told.'

'I have never heard of war tigers,' I said. 'Those beasts are not easy to tame or train.'

'Mahendra's garrison includes a wide variety of wild animals,' said Harisena. 'Leopards. Bears. Wild boars.'

'Wild animals may have novelty and some shock-value but I am not sure how effective they will be in the crush of a real battle where you need training and discipline,' I said.

'They will also use poisoned arrows,' said Harisena.

'That's my biggest worry,' I replied. 'Tell the men they must wear their thickest armour. I know it's hot and it will be very uncomfortable but we cannot afford to take on their arrow shower.'

'Do we take our archers along?' asked Bhasma.

'Maybe a small contingent,' I said. 'This battle will be fought by the infantry and the elephant corps while the cavalry creates a diversion. Remember, their archers will be positioned all along the ramparts and they will be showering us with poisoned arrows. We need to neutralize that firepower with the ferocity and speed of our charge.'

'Jai Garuda,' said Harisena. 'I can hardly wait.'

It was a moonless night but so clear that we could see the Saptarshi constellation spread out like a spangled canopy over us. Apart from the gentle sounds of the river and the rustle of Sal and Mohua leaves around us, all was still. It was as if nature itself stood quiet and expectant, waiting for possibilities to turn up.

A gentle slap-slap in the river told us our nightly visitors were not late. Three tall figures walked up the sand and pebble-strewn riverbank to the small copse that had been cleared for our secret meeting. They came up, dripping water and identified themselves with the tiger-bone pendants strung around their necks. Harisena, always suspicious, body searched them for weapons and then asked for the code word.

'Mahanadi,' said the tallest of the three men.

Harisena nodded and led them to our makeshift meeting place – a bower of creepers so well hidden in the bosom of the forest that even the single earthen lamp that cast a mild glow around it was completely invisible from the outside.

Only one man entered the bower – the tallest and most athletic of the three. He looked at Bhasma and me and bowed, not knowing whom to address.

'Bhima,' he said, simply by way of introduction.

Bhasma, tutored from before, did all the talking. 'We received your message,' he said.

The young man gave a curt nod and looked cautiously at both of us. It was an arresting face, square jawed and high cheekboned, but hidden behind a profusion of tattoos, it looked grotesque even in the half-light. Bhima's slightly bulging eyes moved from Bhasma to me and back to Bhasma in a quick, nervous dance, the only telltale sign of suppressed excitement and agitation. His fleshy lips parted in a slight grimace, showing startling white teeth against the deep brown of his skin. The rest of him – all rippling muscled and long boned – looked like he was carved out of stone. He wore nothing other than a tiger-skin wrap and some bone jewellery on his ears, arms and ankles. His short curly hair was now plastered to his head, sending rivulets of water down his bare body.

'I can help you get inside,' he said.

'How so?' asked Bhasma.

'There's a secret entrance, an escape route,' said Bhima. 'It's known only to members of the royal family. It will take you right inside the palace. After that, it's up to you.'

'And what do you want in return?' asked Bhasma.

'My brother's throne.'

'Any conditions?'

'Don't kill him.'

'Why?'

'Because he's still my brother,' said Bhima.

'How do we know this is not a trap?' asked Bhasma.

The young man shrugged. 'You don't.'

Bhasma looked at me and I half-shook my head.

'We will storm the place anyway,' said Bhasma, 'with or without your help. So if you want us to help *you*, you have to give us some guarantees.'

The young man frowned. 'What kind of guarantees?'

'We will keep you hostage till the raid is over,' said Bhasma. 'After that, we will take you to the city and declare you the king.'

'Sounds like a trap to me,' said Bhima.

'Why should it be?' said Bhasma. 'We are not fighting with you so your life is of no importance to us. Even if we kill you, we still need to fight your brother.'

Bhima thought for a while and then nodded. 'Very well. My men will show you the way. There's a derelict temple in the heart of the jungle on the south side. The tunnel starts there and comes out behind the palace stables.'

'Your men can be trusted, I hope?' asked Bhasma.

'As long as there's enough gold.'

Bhasma smiled. 'It's a deal,' he said.

After that midnight rendezvous, we met Bhima and his cousins several times over the next ten days as Harisena and I turned the plan over and over again between ourselves. My initial reaction was to handle the tunnel charge myself but Harisena refused to allow it. 'We don't know what kind of trap we are walking into,' he said. 'Your life is precious. You are not going anywhere near that tunnel,' he said firmly.

In the meantime, Harisena and a couple of his men had already reconnoitered the tunnel disguised as atavic soldiers. Thankfully, the king's guards who handled the security of the tunnel were severely compromised. Bhima had used the gold we gave him well, and Harisena had no problem going up to the stables and even slipping into the kitchen and servant quarters, the best places to blend in and turn invisible should there be any trouble.

'The palace itself is not particularly well-protected,' said Harisena. 'But it's laid out like a maze. It's a labyrinth of a place, a series of corridors and tunnels that run all over the heart of the fort-city, and unless we know exactly which tunnel to take, it would be impossible to negotiate our way in or out of there.'

'It will be dangerous,' I said. 'Even with Bhima hostage, we will be relying way too much on his men.'

Harisena grinned. 'I want you to lead the diversion on the south side, Majesty,' he said. 'Atop your elephant, silver howdah and all.'

I smiled, getting the drift. 'I will swoop in to breach the south wall, Bhasma will attack from the east, similarly decked out, and the Kosala guards will be too occupied with the twin attack to pay much attention to what's going on inside their palace.'

'Exactly,' said Harisena. 'I will go in and hopefully secure King Mahendra as quickly as possible. That's the only way to neutralize the tunnels, the wild animals and the poisoned darts. We show them we have their king, and force them to capitulate.'

It wasn't a foolproof plan but it was the best we could come up with. 'It should work,' I said, sounding far more confident than I felt.

'It has to,' said Harisena. 'Otherwise we die.'

We began our attack well before dawn, just as the east sky began to pale. We took a longish detour so that we could burst out from the south side in a surprise pre-dawn attack. We had started moving our men and beasts in small consignments over the last few days, doing so in the early hours of the morning and mid-afternoon when the whole world seemed to retreat into a heat-hazed siesta. Harisena grumbled that we always seemed to march in the most unearthly hours, even though the entire troop movement was meticulously planned and executed by him.

It was a beautiful morning, the sky a luminous blue unspoiled by all the fire and gore that was soon to follow. The river rippled pearly grey in the early dawn half-light and all around us nature woke up with a cacophonous chorus, from chattering drongos and chirpy bulbuls to the ubiquitous mynah, and twittering sparrows. Punctuating this symphony were clear intermittent cuckoo calls – some from the bird and some from our men as they assumed position. It was easy to make out the human calls since our signal was two short hoots followed by one long one.

We timed ourselves so that we would emerge at the south gate just before daylight broke. Harisena and his team of twenty brave hearts were already on their way into the heart of the palace led by Bhima's men. The first to break upon the guards on the south side were the archers. They were waiting in the dark and with first light, burst out of the forest cover to shoot fire arrows at the rampart guards. Taken aback, these guards scrambled for cover before coming back to take us on. But that little break was enough time for our catapults to swing into action. They rained fireballs and boulders into the still sleeping city, exploding the peaceful quiet of early dawn to smithereens. Boom, boom, boom. The fireballs hit their targets randomly and efficiently, and suddenly the city burst into a flaming uproar. The rampart guards, not expecting this attack, ran helter-skelter, now taking aim at our advancing elephant corps, and now checking on the pandemonium inside.

Taking advantage of the confusion, I signalled the elephant corps to charge. It began with an ear-splitting symphony as the conch shells rang out, the Dundhubhi and Bheri war drums beat a frenzied rhythm, horses whinnied, elephants trumpeted and men shouted themselves hoarse. Covered in metal-studded leather armour, the beasts swung their heavy iron balls and charged into the southern wall. The battering rams followed close behind, smashing into dents made by the elephant charge. The ground shook. Mounds of earth flew. The rampart started developing an array of cracks. Screams, trumpets, shrill commands and battle drums filled the air. And in between I heard our battle cry, 'Jai Garuda!'

For a mud wall, the rampart held strong much longer than we had expected. Still, by the time the guards gathered their wits and started pouring boiling oil to stave off the charge, a section of the wall had already started to crumble. The elephants were by then in battle frenzy, trumpeting loudly and impaling anything that came their way. But an oil burn is particularly painful and an injured elephant running rampant can decimate any infantry or cavalry. So we pulled back for a while, allowing the rampart guards to sweat off their adrenalin rush. I signalled the archers and the catapult engineers to give us fire cover, and volley after volley of arrow showers and bolts rained out. For a while the exchange of fire was equal as our arrows matched theirs. And then the tides turned.

A section of the rampart guards were still pouring hot oil into the narrow tunnel between the two walls in an effort to keep us from trying to breach the second wall. Suddenly this oil caught fire and before we knew it, the tunnel had burst into flames, causing their guards to hurriedly jump off the rampart. The fire crackled and blazed, and was carried towards the city by the gentle morning breeze. That's when, in the middle of that blazing inferno, I realized that the fight was over. We did not even need to storm the palace. We did not need to breach the wall. All we needed to do was wait for the wind to fan the flames. Fear and confusion would do the rest for us.

In between this carnage, I suddenly heard the clear calls of a cuckoo bird, the pre-arranged signal from Bhasma who was following up with the same manoeuvre on the eastern wall, leading his elephant corps to crash into the mud walls under catapult fire. I signaled my catapult engineers to continue to pummel the city with fire balls – the faster the flames spread, the better. Bhasma too had received similar instructions. He was to attack the wall and then rain a shower of fire balls to distract the guards. It was all going according to plan. The only question mark right now was the ambush and kidnapping of King Mahendra. If Harisena managed that cleanly, we would be able to wrap up the fighting before mid-day.

Amidst the tumult, a steady lineup of informants brought me news from the eastern wall. It seemed the sudden attack on two fronts took the Kosala guards completely by surprise. While they were expecting an attack and were tracking our troop and baggage movement day by day, they had no idea how fleet-footed our battle charge could be. The day prior they had seen us across the river where my reserves still kept up appearances, completely confusing the Kosala scouts following our trail. Meanwhile half my men had moved upstream, crossed the river, cut through a detour and landed on their southern and eastern doorsteps backed by elephants and horsemen.

Despite the surprise element, Bhasma did not find it easy to breach those walls. The doors had spikes and after the initial confusion, the guards took position on the ramparts releasing volley after volley of poisoned arrows. The arrows did not bother the elephants too much – they were well protected by their leather and metal armour – but it did take a toll on our foot soldiers. Several battering rams had to be discarded as men fell to poisoned arrows and once the hot oil and boulder shower began, our elephants had to pull back too.

Fortunately for Bhasma, there was too much happening for the Kosala guards to focus attention on only one front. The city was on fire, its residents running helter-skelter and there was complete bedlam everywhere. Bhasma and I made sure no one could get out of the blazing fortress – any one who tried was greeted with our arrow shower. The stalemate continued for nearly two hours, my anxiety rising with every passing moment. Our catapults were running out of ammunition and our archers were running out of arrows. If Harisena did not manage to secure the king before the fires died out, we'd be in trouble. Worse, if Harisena was captured by the enemy, he would be used to dictate terms in the negotiation. It would be a mess.

I tried to retain my outward calm but my insides were quivering with trepidation. I cursed myself for allowing my best friend to go into that tunnel. Now I didn't even know whether Harisena was dead or alive. I didn't know whether our biggest bargain had turned into our costliest mistake. I gripped my sword hilt and prayed. I prayed for Harisena. I prayed for Datta and our unborn future. I prayed for myself.

That's when I heard Harisena's Panchajanya ring out loud and clear from the thick forests behind us. It was the signal we were waiting for. The signal that told us Harisena had captured King Mahendra.

The battle was over.

11
Kosala and Maha Kantar

'HE RAN INTO OUR arms, Majesty,' said Harisena. 'The coward was running away from his people and walked straight into our ambush.'

The battle was over but the stories went on and on.

'No, no this won't do,' I said. 'You must tell me from the beginning.'

Harisena smiled, tweaking the ends of his moustache as he reached out for a mango from the fruit platter in front of him. Small and rosy, they looked different from the ones back home but were deliciously juicy. You didn't need to cut these open to take the stone out. You could nip off a side and simply suck on them.

'Well, despite everything, I couldn't bring myself to trust Bhima's men completely,' he said. 'So instead of kidnapping King Mahendra from his palace, I decided to wait for him in the tunnel itself.'

'What made you change your mind? I mean, how could you know for sure that he would bolt and that too right into the tunnel?' asked Bhasma.

'The archers are my men,' said Harisena. 'They kept me informed about how the southern and eastern charge fared. If things did not go our way, I would have gone in and tried to kidnap the king as earlier planned. But the fire made all the difference. This was his only escape.'

'Yes, the gods were with us on that day,' I said. 'When the fire broke out, I wanted to send you a signal but didn't know how.'

Harisena turned to me, his eyes smiling. 'You needn't have worried. I had to know what was going on so I could tweak my plans accordingly. When the fire broke out, we held back. I told my men to position themselves all along the tunnel but not stop anyone trying to escape from the palace. I tracked the fire and waited for the king to blink. Bhima's men had told us that the fort inside is like a maze. With a fire raging, it would turn into a death trap. There was no way Mahendra would risk it. He would run. All we needed to do was wait for him to come to us.'

'Now that we have him under our thumb, what do we do with him?' asked Bhasma.

'Nothing,' I replied.

Harisena looked up, surprised. 'Aren't we going to install Bhima in his place?'

I shook my head. 'Absolutely not. Bhima is a traitor. I cannot have that adharma on my head.'

'But you promised,' said Bhasma.

'No, *you* promised,' I replied. 'I did nothing. Bhima gave us access and we paid for it with gold. I owe him nothing more.'

'But this could endanger his life,' said Harisena.

'I have spoken to King Mahendra,' I replied, 'and made the terms of the treaty very clear to him. He has agreed to three things. First, he will announce fealty to my Garuda Dhwaja and accept my suzerainty in open court. He will pay us a yearly tax in return for our protection. Second, he will allow us to use Kosala as a base to launch an attack on Maha Kantar and further south. Third, he will not hurt Bhima in any way. If he does, he will have me to contend with.'

'And in return?' asked Bhasma.

'He will continue as the King of Kosala. I have no desire to annex his kingdom.'

'But we won the battle,' said Bhasma. 'So why not annex?'

'Because it is too far for us to hold.'

'So why fight then?'

'So that, in future, King Mahendra will know his place. He will know that he owes his throne to me and I can take it away any time I want. It will keep things in perspective. And stop him from undertaking any kind of misadventure by himself or in collusion with others.'

'So all this for a deterrent,' said Bhasma, in a small voice.

'All this for the future,' I replied.

Bhasma lowered his head. 'I know you feel bad about Bhima,' I said. 'But remember, no legitimate ruler will ever back a usurper. It's against the divine order of kingship. I can use any means I like – fair or foul – to win a war. That doesn't mean I trust those who betray their own.'

'Nor should you,' said Harisena, as much to Bhasma as to me.

We spent the next couple of weeks in Shripur settling the new order in and allowing our men to rest and recuperate. King Mahendra proved to be a willing ally, helping replenish our arrow and catapult bolts, and offering scouts to take us to Maha Kantar through a shorter jungle route. Asurgarh was just a couple of days ride from Shripur and I wanted to set out as quickly as possible. We were less than four weeks away from the rainy month of Ashar and I wanted to wrap up the Maha Kantar campaign well before the rains turned the terrain sludgy and impassable.

King Mahendra's generosity apart, the Kosala campaign turned out to be a bigger boon for us than I had ever imagined. The Shripur fort had a formidable reputation as impregnable and news of our victory in that battle spread quickly through the length and breadth of Dakshinapath.

'The bards are already singing about it, sire,' said Harisena. 'They say it takes a god to take down a bolt hole like Shripur.'

I laughed. 'I hope our friend Byagra is listening too.'

'Asurgarh is protected by a deep lake, a river and a moat infested with crocodiles. I don't know how we're going to land up at his doorstep in a surprise raid like we did here,' said Bhasma.

'It will have to be a siege, I suppose,' said Harisena. 'Except we don't have time on our side.'

'Our best bet is to intimidate him into submission,' I said. 'King Mahendra has already written to him telling him in no uncertain terms that Kosala has done atma nivedan to

Magadh and any plans Byagra has to take us on will have to exclude Kosala.'

'That means he's left without an ally,' said Bhasma. 'And is facing a formidable army led by a god. He should blink.'

'I am counting on that,' I replied. 'But if he doesn't, this won't be an easy one to win.'

Asurgarh took my breath away. It sat like a pearl surrounded by water, glimmering under angry grey rain clouds that cast a blue tinge on the green ridges to the west. The Sandul River, impetuous and already swollen with rainwater, flowed past its western rampart. On the east, as far as the eye could see, stretched a lake, a sheet of rippling water that seemed to merge with the far horizon. The fort itself was a roughly square-build structure, stone based and brick laid. It was surrounded by a moat on its north and south where, our Kosala guides informed us, Byagra kept his pet crocodiles. The fort had four gates, each with its own guardian diety – Ganga on the east, Dokri on the south, Kalapat on the west and Vaishnavi on the north.

'It *is* beautiful,' whispered Harisena, almost under his breath.

'And very well protected by nature and man,' added Bhasma.

'I am hoping he'll lose his nerve,' said Harisena. 'The nor'westers are threatening to break any time now and I don't particularly want to camp out in the open in the middle of a thunder storm.'

I didn't reply but I could see Harisena's point. Despite scouts, guides, ammunition and logistic help from

Mahendra, this fort could be near impossible to breach. Now rain-fed, the river looked angry and fording it would be extremely difficult. Besides, the fort was very well protected on the east thanks to the lake so our only option was to risk the crocodiles, cross the moat and attack the northern or southern gates. Even if the infantry and cavalry managed it with sheer speed, it would have to do so without the elephants and the catapults – both too bulky and cumbersome to risk crossing a moat brimming with crocodiles. But without elephants and catapult slingshots, we would be seriously hobbled in terms of attack options.

Kosala's scouts had cleared up a large swathe of forest on the southern side and set up camp for us. But looking at the grey clouds swirling above, I directed my men to fell more trees and raise a palisade. We would need more than flimsy camps if we were to stick it out in this weather even for a week. We had to send out a message to Byagra that we weren't going to budge come rain or sun. It was the only way to cower him into submission. Otherwise, we were looking at a long, rain-soaked, fever-infested siege ahead.

To be honest, things did not start well for us. Despite help from our Kosala friends, it still took the men nearly a week to set up camp and they had to battle a couple of vicious storms while they were at it. Still, by the end of it, they did a decent enough job. The palisade looked pretty stout and inside the men raised wood-and-thatch huts on stilts to keep us and our supplies dry if the river were to flood. The thick forests meant there was plenty of game and fodder for everyone and Bhasma kept himself occupied by routinely going out with our foraging teams to hunt for the pot. Though not a stone and brick fortification, our palisade looked much sturdier than the usual battle camp, prompting Bhasma to wonder whether we would spend the entire rainy season crocodile spotting at Asurgarh.

'Aren't you sending him an envoy to check things out?' asked Harisena.

'Not yet,' I said. 'Give him any indication that we are in a hurry to wrap this up quickly, and he'll simply sit tight and wait us out. Remember, he's inside, nice, dry and cozy, and we'll be out here battling the elements. No, no. This is a battle of nerves. We can't afford to blink first.'

Harisena's brow arched into a question mark. 'What if he doesn't blink at all?'

I clapped him on the back. 'He's never won even a skirmish against Magadh. Trust me, he'll break.'

'Can't we starve them out?' asked Bhasma.

'With a river on one side and a lake on the other? I don't think so. There's enough fish in there to feed them for the next month or two.'

For a while, all three of us chewed on the situation. I was convinced Byagra would blink but the only question was when.

'He doesn't need to fight – flood, fever and frustration will do his job nicely enough,' said Bhasma. It was something none of us wanted to think about – the possibility that Byagra would take his own sweet time to come around. And as the weeks rolled on and the rain clouds burst upon us, Bhasma's words began to sound more and more prophetic. Despite our best efforts, the camp soon turned into a marshland. Both men and animals died of snakebites and fever. Foraging became difficult in the incessant downpour. And the River Sandul was in spate – if the flooding got worse, our scouts warned us, the camp would be in waist-high water.

'We are losing men every day,' complained Bhasma. 'How long do we wait for Byagra to run scared?'

'Let us go back to Kosala, sire,' said Harisena. 'Wait out the rainy months. We can come back at the beginning of Bhadra (mid-August).

'If we blink now, we will never defeat Byagra,' I said. 'We have to stare him down. There's no other way.'

The days crept by one by one, dripping despair as more and more men fell prey to the shivering fever. We began to lose horses too though King Mahendra assured us he would send fresh supplies once the rains let up. By the beginning of Shravan (mid-July), we had been camping in that godforsaken site for nearly five weeks and morale was about as low as it could get. The men were desperate for action – any action – and even Harisena began to grumble that the lull would kill him if the mosquito bites did not. And then, Bhasma fell ill.

He'd gone hunting as usual but came back drenched and shivering. By nightfall, his body was on fire. The camp physicians kept a small bowl of camphor burning day and night in his sleeping quarters. They massaged his feet with warm oil, bathed his forehead and armpits, and covered the rest of him in quilts that smelt musty in the soggy weather. The fever raged on for three full days. On the fourth, the royal physician gave me the bad news. 'If the fever doesn't break in the next twenty-four hours, we could lose him, Majesty,' he said.

I took Harisena aside and told him to send an envoy to Byagra for help. 'I can't risk losing Bhasma,' I told him.

'His mother will blame it all on you,' replied Harisena.

'Forget about his mother,' I snapped. '*I* will blame it all on me.'

The next morning the charcoal sky looked so unforgiving that my heart sank. Bhasma was still delirious. The weather was angry. All hope, as far as I could see, was lost. And yet, just as our messenger trotted up to ride out, I saw a thin sliver of light break through the dark clouds. Moments later, a group of men, wearing the grass skirts and green laurels typical of Byagra's tribe, rode up to our camp. It was a peace offering. The shivering fever had claimed more than a dozen lives inside the fort, the last being Byagra's youngest and favourite son. The Tiger King had lost his appetite for a fight. He was ready to talk.

That afternoon, Bhasma's fever broke.

We camped at Asurgarh for the remaining rainy months. I wanted to plan the next leg of the campaign and for that I needed the scouts to map the terrain first. Once he offered his fealty, Byagra proved to be a helpful ally, offering us his fort for shelter as well as his seasoned forest scouts to help chart the route. I wanted to hug the coast all the way down to Kanchi but I had only a sketchy idea of the topography and terrain. The scouts helped me work it out.

The first kingdom on our list was Kurala, ruled by Manta Raja. This lay to the south of Kosala and would give us access to the rich and very fertile land between two great rivers – Mahanadi and Godavari. This stretch was ruled by three kings – Mahendragiri of Pishtapura on the east of the Godavari river, Swamidatta of Kottura near Kalinga (modern Ganjam district) and Kubera of Devarashtra closer to the coast. All three were relatively small kingdoms but together they held the land that would give me access to the deep South. Harisena suggested he would go ahead and parley with them. After our resounding victory at Kosala and Byagra's very public surrender, it would not be difficult to cower them into subjugation. Since we were demanding nothing more than an atma nivedan and a yearly tax, I reasoned, it would not be difficult to make these rulers see sense.

South of this region lay a number of kingdoms, some big, others small. This was the land hugged by three mighty rivers – Godavari in the north, Krishna in the south and Tungabhadra in the southwest. The kings who ruled this land included Dhananjaya of Kushthalapura whose kingdom lay between Godavari and Krishna, Hastivarman of Vengi on the banks of the Krishna, and Damana of Erandapalla, west of the Godavari. Beyond this was Nilaraja's realm Avamukta on the banks of the Tungabhadra from where we would march in a southeasterly direction towards Palakka, King Ugrasena's kingdom, just a day's ride from Kanchi.

From what our spies told us, it was clear we would have to fight our way through most of this area. These southern kings were rich and enjoyed good neighbourly relations with each other. Which meant even smaller kingdoms would not give up their suzerainty without a fight, knowing that their allies would back them up.

'We could face a confederacy,' said Harisena.

I agreed that was entirely possible. But with Byagra and Mahendra supplying horses, elephants and pack animals, we now had a base to venture forth into this very prosperous land whose glittering temples and beautifully carved Viharas were known all over Jamvudweep.

'My spies tell me King Ugrasena of Palakka is a Pallava prince who is a distant kinsman of both regent Vishnugopa as well as his nephew, the boy king Skanda Varman,' said Harisena.

'Which means...' I asked.

'If we attack him, Kanchi will step forward to help,' said Harisena.

I smiled. 'We draw them out and take them on in one fell swoop ... I like that.'

Harisena's eyes glinted. 'We could do that. Or you could simply marry Angai and make a kinsman out of an enemy.'

I looked straight into his eyes. They did not reflect the smile on his lips.

'For the last time, I am not doing this for Angai,' I said. 'I am doing this for myself and for the future of my legacy. If you must carry tales to Datta, just make sure you carry the right ones.'

12

Blue Beyond

THE ROAR RANG IN my ears and my eyes were full of blue. The sun-kissed water sprayed salt and foam on my face. I was riding the wind. I was ruling the waves. Tantalizing and tempestuous, an exquisite expanse spread out before me. A rainbow of colours, all blue – inky blue, sky blue, aqua marine, grey blue ... Crowned by the white surf, the waves swept me on and on. I knew not where. I knew not why. Perhaps the where and why didn't matter after all. What did was what I saw all around – an infinity, stretching from horizon to heaven. Limitless in its promise. Relentless in its call. Primeval, powerful, pure.

The dream drew me in like a swirling vortex. My reality obliterated, I was sucked into the deepest abyss of that teeming azure. I drowned in my wakefulness. I woke up dreaming. My feet in the golden sand, the sun in my eyes, I gazed at the sapphire waves crashing at my feet. Kanchi. After a lifetime of waiting, I had reached the ocean's edge.

I no longer needed to hold a conch shell to hear the waves. Their roar rang in my ear, that brilliant blue filled my soul. I closed my eyes and lifted my face to this swirling swathe. I tasted the salt on my tongue. The brine and seaweed filled my nose. It felt like salvation.

The gentle footsteps behind brought me back to reality. 'They want to parley, sire,' Harisena whispered into my ear.

I turned around to face him. The campaign had changed Harisena visibly, his earlier athletic frame was now positively wiry and there were fine lines around his eyes and the corners of his mouth. His bronze skin was now deeply sunburnt and his lovingly tended to moustache was gone, replaced by a grizzled unkempt stubble. He looked much older than his age. Perhaps I did too but in the rough and tumble of a campaign, I had neither the desire nor the respite to look into a mirror. Maybe I wasn't ready for what I would see, if I did.

It had been more than nine months since we set out from Pataliputra. My southern sojourn would not have been possible without my best friend by my side. He used a mix of deft diplomacy and threat to cower the Kalinga confederacy of Pishtapura, Kottura and Devarashtra into submission. And it was his quick thinking that helped save the day when we faced the formidable southern alliance of Kushthalapura, Vengi and Erandapalla on the banks of the River Krishna. One by one, they bent their knee to the Garuda Dhwaja just like I dreamt they would. I had planned to wrap up the rest of the campaign well before Agrayan (mid-December), when the rain clouds move south causing giant waves, fearsome tempests and massive flooding. Also, I was eager to go back ever since word arrived from Pataliputra that Datta had delivered a healthy baby boy. My mother had named him Rama Gupta. Just like that, I was now a father and suddenly the only thing that mattered was to rush back home and hold the child in my arms.

But things weren't going as planned on this last leg of our campaign. The Pallavas were proving surprisingly difficult to overcome. King Ugrasena of Palakka had asked for help from his Pallava kinsmen in Kanchi, just as we had expected him to. That blood-drenched battle lasted two entire days but threw up no clear winner. In the end, Ugrasena had withdrawn into his fort and we had no option but to lay siege to it.

That was more than four weeks ago. Vishnugopa, the regent of Kanchi – expecting a similar treatment for helping his neighbour and kinsman – also withdrew into his city. I divided my force into two halves: Bhasma leading the Palakka siege and Harisena and I handling the Kanchi one. Fortunately for us, the weather held up. The skies remained cheerfully azure. The waves stayed tame and the weather sun-kissed and balmy. My men dug a makeshift trench around the city to wait out the enemy's patience. We fished and hunted, held jousts and war games. And waited for the food to run out in Kanchi.

For the first ten days, both sides waited for the other to blink. Located on the banks of the Vegavathy River, the city had no shortage of water and initially small coracle boats would venture out fishing, well beyond the reach of our arrow shower from the opposite bank. Harisena began to grumble that we would have to wait for the river to run out of fish if we wanted to starve Kanchi into submission.

I knew their grain wouldn't last forever but I had no desire to continue the siege indefinitely. Although the weather was still surprisingly dry, we were dangerously close to the stormy southern winter. And I felt we were tempting fate by prolonging what should have been a quick day-long raid, at best. Bhasma too wasn't having much luck with his campaign and for a while it looked like a stalemate.

And then, once again, the goddess of fortune smiled upon us. A trading hub, Kanchi's population included merchants from across Jamvudeep and beyond. At any given point, Roman sura wine sellers jostled with Chinese monks and Persian horse traders while Jewish caravans occupied the parking lot just outside the city. Known for its fine cotton and silk weaving, Kanchi exported its wares not only to many kingdoms up north, but also to such faraway places as China, Babylon and Egypt. The trade made this cosmopolitan melting pot of a city very rich. But it also made Kanchi particularly vulnerable to disease. Plagues and pestilences travelled by boat and were carried into the city by infected visitors. The citizens mostly reacted with alacrity at the first signs of any sickness by instantly throwing out the infected persons as a quarantine measure. The trouble however is that a quarantine is impossible to impose under a military siege.

We first heard of the pox through our foraging scouts. It seemed the Naga traders who carried it into the city had kept things quiet for a while. But when the infected started to die, news spread like wild fire within the compounds. The authorities could not dump the bodies in the river for fear of infecting the water. So when they ran out of firewood for the pyres, the bodies were buried hurriedly all along the eastern ramparts that bordered the city's grazing grounds. But as the infection spread rapidly, the dead began to pile up and the merchant guilds that controlled the commerce in this city of silk and gold began to push for peace.

Vishnugopa was caught between commerce and conscience. The guilds were backed by the city's biggest temples, which effectively bankrolled much of the silk trade. Unless the epidemic was controlled, Kanchi would lose both lives and livelihoods. Without the taxes that the trade brought in, the city would not be able to afford an army, much less wage a war. But bending his knee to the imperial Garuda Dhwaja meant ceding suzerainty. As regent, Vishnugopa was loathe to give away a kingdom that was not his by right.

It belonged to his nephew and he, Vishnugopa, was merely its trustee. As long as he lived, he could not shun his duty towards his ward. So far, he had resolutely fobbed off all efforts at a rapprochement. Despite persistent pleas by the likes of King Dhananjaya of Kushthalapura, King Hastivarman of Vengi and King Damana of Erandapalla – all part of the defeated confederacy of southern rulers who were now helping us with supplies and diplomatic effort – the Pallava regent stuck to his point that the kingdom of Kanchi was not his to give up.

But now that resolve seemed to be crumbling. Kanchi's willingness to talk meant they were desperate. And that could only be good news for us. I clapped Harisena on the back and said, 'It's always good to talk. Ask them to send their man. Let's parley.'

Harisena refused to meet my eye. 'Their envoy is waiting for you, Majesty. It's someone you already know.'

I frowned. 'I don't think I have personally met Regent Vishnugopa,' I said. 'And their king, Skanda Varman, is a child.'

'Kanchi's envoy is Princess Angai,' said Harisena. 'Parley, sire?'

She glittered like a jewel in the golden glare of a mid-morning sun. A profusion of rubies and emeralds glinted around her neck and covered her torso – an exquisite armour that chained in the pleats of her blood red *chinanshuk* sari with military precision. A wide gold belt accentuated her slender waist and thick ropes of mogra jasmine twisted themselves all along her long, tight braid. She walked in, hips gently swaying like a dancer, her golden anklets tinkling on the carpeted floor, holding a bunch of red and white long-stemmed lotus blooms in her hand. I stole a glance at Harisena and saw the familiar questioning arch on his brow. Was Angai here to talk or seduce me into peace?

'This is a surprise,' I said. 'I wasn't expecting you, princess.'

'I could say the same to you, Majesty,' she replied, and then held out the flowers for me. 'Welcome to Kanchi.'

'This is a battlefield, madam,' said Harisena brusquely. 'We have no use for flowers.'

'It is good to greet friends with civility, is it not?' she asked. 'Besides, I brought these flowers simply to thank His Majesty for keeping his promise.'

I smiled. 'You remember,' I said.

She flashed a dimpled grin. 'You are by far the best student I have ever taught. How could I forget?'

I heard a soft grunt from Harisena. 'Wonderful. If all else fails, we could decide this through a Silambam match,' he said.

I nodded. 'Of course, even though my lessons are far from complete.'

'That can be easily fixed,' she replied smoothly. 'I will start giving you lessons as long as you are here.'

'Be careful, princess,' I replied. 'It may keep me back longer than necessary.'

'Be careful, Majesty,' she smiled. 'It may keep you back forever.'

'Sounds like a promise,' I joked.

'Not to me,' whispered Harisena.

The war council began the parley as soon as the priests had blessed the gathering. In public, Angai looked proud and aloof with no signs of the teasing intimacy that we shared when she greeted me with the flowers. She sat straight, her head held high and her face carved into inscrutability.

'Well, madam?' I asked. 'Has your brother given you the authority to discuss the terms of surrender?'

'My brother has given me permission to talk,' she replied calmly. 'I told him I made your acquaintance in Mathura and this whole debacle may, in fact, be the result of some small misunderstanding.'

'Small misunderstanding?' asked Harisena.

'My presence in Mathura was not the result of some hush-hush alliance that Kanchi was hoping to forge with the Naga kings up north. The Nagas have been our friends for centuries. Indeed, the first Pallava king, our revered forefather, was the offspring of Sage Ashwathama and a

Naga princess. The royal Pallavas are related to the Nagas by blood. There's no conspiracy there.'

'Wonderful,' whispered Harisena. 'A history lesson in the middle of war.'

Angai turned her long neck and pierced him with a glare. 'History can be very educative to those who care to learn from it.'

Harisena shrugged away that barb. 'I am sure you're not here to discuss history, madam. If you are, I suggest you return to your pox-ridden city. Unfortunately, we are in the middle of a battle. We don't have time for such enlightened intellectual pursuits.'

Angai turned her imperious gaze towards me. 'My people are dying of plague and starvation. My beautiful city is sinking under the debris of death. Why cause this needless suffering? What do you gain by this?'

'I don't want this any more than you do,' I replied. 'But I am not the one refusing diplomacy. Maybe you should talk some sense into your brother.'

'This land is not my brother's to bargain away,' she said. 'It would be adharma to do so.'

'What kind of dharma dictates that you watch your people die because you cannot get off the fence,' snapped Harisena. 'It's time Regent Vishnugopa stopped wringing his hands and took some action. Hiding behind the city gates was not such a great idea after all.'

'I have come here to parley,' retorted Angai, in a voice as sharp as a sword blade. 'But I will only do so with a monarch of the blood.'

I glanced at Harisena. He looked frustrated but held his tongue. 'I have no problems parleying,' I said. 'Tell your brother I am willing to talk. Let's see what he can offer us that we cannot snatch away by sword.'

Angai dropped her gaze and for a few moments there was silence in the room. Then she said, 'My brother respects and reveres you, Majesty, just like the rest of Jamvudeep. Come to us in friendship and we will take you to our heart. But do not push us to the wall. If you do, we will have no option but to fight back.'

'Fight back with what?' interrupted Harisena. 'You must agree, madam, that your position in this exchange is somewhat compromised. Your people are starving and dying of the pox. Your city is surrounded and your allies have deserted you. You have nowhere to turn except to the Garuda Dhwaja.'

Angai's eyes flashed fire. 'As far as I know, my kinsmen are still holding out in Palakka, just as we are in Kanchi. The pox will die out and this balmy weather will not hold. When the tempest hits you with the vicious force of 10,000 war elephants, when the kadal kol (destructive wave/tsunami) devours the land, scattering your men and animals, destroying your camp and wrecking your battle plans, it is you who will want to parley. I am not negotiating from a position of weakness. I belong to this land. I know it better than you ever will. If you want to spend the rest of the winter outside our city gates, be my guest,' she snapped.

'A real and present plague as opposed to an imagined storm?' sneered Harisena. 'I'll take my chances.'

'Tell your brother we are willing to wait for him to come to his senses,' I said. 'When he does, come back here. We'll talk.'

She caught up with me on my morning ride to the edge of the ocean. For the longest time, she was just a speck in the horizon but as she came closer, I recognized the blood red sari and the glint of rubies and emeralds she had around her throat and wrist. Her black mare was frothing at the mouth as she rode up next to me, pulling back the reigns to slow her to a gentler trot. I looked at her and raised my eyebrows in question. 'Isn't it too soon for another parley?' I asked.

'Just a chat,' she smiled and replied.

'Race me to the ocean front?' I asked. 'If you win, I promise to listen to whatever you have to say.'

'Done,' she grinned, and before I could react spurred her mount to a quick gallop to gain momentum. 'Catch me if you can,' she shouted as the black mare shot off like an arrow, a blurred dot gaining distance with every passing moment.

I loosened the reigns and allowed my horse to pick up speed. As I raised myself on the saddle and used my knees to spur him on, I could feel every sinew in his taut chestnut body heave and ebb. I had the sun in my eyes, the wind running through my hair and the salty tang of the ocean on my tongue. I felt my being soar. *I was riding the wind. I was ruling the waves.* I was the ocean's own and my destiny was just a short trot away. Nothing could stop me. Nothing would.

On and on we rode, through the flat gold-green fields, their paddy crop ripe for the winter harvest. Punctuated by the occasional copse of coconut and palm trees, and hemmed in the far distance by grey-blue hillocks that reflected the cloudless blue of the sky above, this carpet of yellowish-green swayed in the gentle breeze quite unaware of the death and starvation within the city walls. The golden sunshine warmed our souls and dripped off our sweat-stained backs. The tumult and tension of the campaign slowly drained away and I could breathe lightly once more. I was Lichchavidauhitra Kacha again, dreaming about a future written in the stars. My past and future melted away in that gold-drenched morning and all that remained was the present. A glorious, sun-kissed present.

My horse had settled into a brisk gallop but I spurred him on to go faster. Angai was already half a kos ahead of me and I could see the blood-red pallu flying like a pennant behind her. I missed Pushpak, my beautiful grey mount whom Angai had injured fatally in Mathura. The horse I was riding now – while a decent animal – did not share that instinctive bond that bound Pushpak to me. Angai, on the other hand, was riding her own mount and she also had a head start by a minute or two. I would have to push harder to catch up.

The paddy fields thinned out into coconut and palm groves, and the soil below turned from bright red-brown to a sandy dust and finally to yellow sand. I could smell the waves. I could taste the salty tang. And then I saw it. Heaven held earth in a cerulean embrace. The blue horizon rippled under the warm winter sun. Angai was a red spec in the distance as I spurred my horse to go faster and faster and faster. My eyes were full of blue and all that mattered was the call of the ocean. *Primal, powerful, pure.*

The horses slowed down in the sandy beach and we slid off our saddles and raced to the water's edge. Angai waded in, beckoning me to follow. The waves crashed at our feet, covering them with sand. I walked in further, looking for a firmer grip on that shifting ground, finding none and getting pulled in deeper. Then a giant wave hit and before I knew it, I was lying flat on my back, cradled in the briny water, trying to hold onto something to haul myself up again. I reached out blindly and found a hand that pulled me to my feet. I scrambled up and looked into a pair of smiling eyes. 'The ocean can bring the mightiest to their knees,' she joked. 'And she often does.'

'That's why I want to be like her,' I said. 'I am the ocean's own.'

'You should call yourself Samudragupta,' she said.

'Maybe I will. Once I plant the Garuda Dhwaja on this land.'

The smile faded. 'Why is it so important?' she asked.

'I came here, you know. Many years ago. I made a promise to the ocean. I told her I would return. And when I did, I would claim her for myself.'

There it was, that slight tilt of the head again, as if she half-agreed but not quite. And then she said, 'You can't conquer her, you know. You can only surrender, with love.'

'Love can conquer too,' I said.

'True devotion comes from surrender,' she replied.

We stood facing each other as the waves crashed into us, willing us to dive in, drown in the briny surf and roll in the sand. I was the first to tumble, rolling in the wet sand, allowing the waves to wash over me, surrendering myself body and soul to the call of the blue. I closed my eyes and opened myself to that moment of exhilaration. And then I felt her in my arms.

Her sari wrapped itself around me, her arms clung to my neck while her lips found mine. She tasted of the ocean – wild and wonderful, part woman, part wave, untamed and fierce, primal and pure. I was awash with ecstasy. Eyes closed, I let my lips find her; the hollow of her throat, the swell of her nipples, the dent of her navel, the soft, wet desire of her womanhood. She moaned in my ears, it sounded like the roar of the waves. I drowned in her hunger and I lost myself in her release. I was riding the waves, deeper and deeper till I was one with its primal call. I was swept into a vortex of swirling euphoria. I lay back utterly spent and surrendered myself to this force of nature.

'Conquer?' she whispered in my ear.

'Surrender,' I replied and buried myself in her.

13
Kadal Kol

THE STORM CAME SUDDENLY. The sea turned a swirling seething grey, the sky matched it tone for tone and a shrill wind began to blow. Our scouts told us to hunker down for the big one. It hit just before dawn, the roaring, howling wind ripping through our camp, scattering the pack animals and blowing away the fencing. I had never seen anything like this in my life. Summer storms could be vicious too, but this was something else. Elemental in its fury, unpredictable in its moods, it crashed through branches, forced the upright coconut trees to bend in deference and turned houses into rubble. The wind whipped up waves that were as high as hillocks. Frothing white, they crashed on the shore, their rage spilling over, dousing the sand and clawing back anything that stood in its way.

We would have faced the full blast of its wrath had we kept to our camp. But on the advice of our local scouts, we had moved to a fishing village further inland, using their mud and thatch huts to keep ourselves and our animals as dry as possible. The horses whinnied in nervousness, the elephants bellowed, adding to the roar of the elements outside. The storm burst upon us in a savage swirl that blurred the world around us. On and on it raged, for nearly two *prahars* and then, just as suddenly, the wind dropped. The sky looked scrubbed clean, the sun came out and the waves calmed down. But for the devastation we saw all around, it could have just been a bad dream.

Later we walked into the wreckage that was once our camp. Everything was in tatters; nothing had been spared. Only those who took refuge in the siege ditch had survived. The storm had hit us hard. We lost a few men but we lost many more pack animals. Harisena and his men got to work immediately, trying to salvage what they could from the debris. By dusk, only a few flimsy canopies were up and we spent the night wondering if the storm would return.

That was when Vishnugopa decided to push for peace. The storm had hurt us much more than him. The city's stone and brick houses were far sturdier and its high walls helped break the path of the wind, reducing its power to destroy. He had guessed, rightly, that morale would be low among my men. So even before we could clean up the campsite and rebuild it, there came the offer for another parley.

They picked their way through the detritus and I saw a faint smile on Angai's lips. She looked around – taking in the extent of the destruction with what seemed to be obvious satisfaction – and occasionally put a quiet word to her brother who walked beside her. Vishnugopa's face was grim. He wrapped his uttaria scarf tighter around his lean torso and refused to look up. For a royal regent, he was modestly dressed, giving no indication of Kanchi's famed wealth. He wore a white silk antariya dhoti and no jewellery at all. His wide patrician forehead, smeared with holy ash and vermillion, was furrowed with deep creases. He could see what the storm did to us but unlike Angai, he wasn't at all sure it would make us change our mind.

When we sat down to talk, his sharp grey eyes flitted warily from me to Harisena to Angai. Thin lips, pursed in a straight line of perpetual disapproval, remained unsmiling. He was pleading for detente but didn't look like he relished the idea.

'Majesty, we can resolve this through peaceful means,' he said. 'Like I said before, I revere you and would be honoured to host you in my humble city. I can see how badly the storm has hurt you. You have doubtless lost men and property, and we wish to offer you our warm hospitality,' he said.

'I thank you,' I replied. 'The storm was nasty but we have weathered much worse on this campaign. We will accept your kind offer only when you accept our Garuda protection.'

Angai looked up and I saw the surprise in her eyes. 'This is the season for stormy weather,' she said. 'You have seen the destruction it can cause. Can you afford to weather out another one? And then another? And yet another?'

'Are we talking about the weather or the war?' asked Harisena.

'We are talking about what's best for both of us,' said Vishnugopa. 'I do not wish another storm on you. So why would you wish plague and famine on my people?'

'I don't,' I said. 'You can end the siege this moment. Accept my suzerainty. Embrace me in friendship. If you lock swords with me, I have no option but to crush you.'

'Majesty, you say you bear us no ill will. We have never molested you or yours in any way. So why do you want my city to suffer?' asked Angai, soft enough to sound like a personal plea but loud enough to carry to her brother sitting next to her.

I was getting tired of this unending circle of reason and counter-reason. The offer for a parley came from them but so far Vishnugopa had given no indication that he understood the gravity of his situation. He clearly thought he could sweet-talk me into lifting the siege simply because of a storm. I turned to Angai and looked straight into her eyes. She had assured me that her brother was open to all possibilities. What was she playing at?

'I thought we had made ourselves clear the last time you came with a peace offering, madam,' I told her. 'If your brother is unwilling to see reason, is there any point to all this?'

Angai's face flushed at the public rebuke but she didn't reply. Vishnugopa's lips almost disappeared in a forbidding grimace.

'If I may be so bold,' he said, 'I am sorry my sister promised more than she was permitted to. She told me you were willing to talk. That's why we are here.'

'Clearly you are not open to seeing reason yet,' interjected Harisena. 'Your people are dying, your city is plagued by sickness and famine, and yet you cannot bring yourself to submit to the Garuda protection. No matter, we can wait. Till you come to your senses.'

I saw a glint in those cold grey eyes but the face remained impassive. 'Death or dishonour,' whispered Vishnugopa. 'It's not much of a choice.'

'There's no dishonour in accepting the emperor's protection,' insisted Harisena. 'Your neighbours have done it, willingly and gratefully. But you seem bent on self-destruction.'

'They had their own compulsions,' he said, more to himself. 'I have mine.'

'If you cannot decide for your people, what right do you have to rule over them?' I asked.

'I ask myself that question every day, Majesty,' he replied. 'But I am afraid I have no answer.'

'If you cannot decide, allow His Highness Skanda Varman to do so,' said Harisena. 'I am told he is an exceptionally intelligent young man. Let him decide.'

'He is only eleven years old,' said Angai. 'When he is ready to decide for himself, he will be ready to rule as well.'

'Still, he is old enough to see what your intransigence is doing to his people. Does he approve of what you're doing in his name?' I asked.

Brother and sister greeted this question with a sullen silence that spoke more eloquently than all the words that had been uttered that afternoon.

Harisena looked at me and I nodded. 'We are this close to a breakthrough in Palakka,' he said. 'Your kinsman has sent word; he is willing to negotiate. Think about that the next time you come to parley and maybe you'll find it in yourself to be more reasonable.'

Vishnugopa's proud chin was up. Defiance flashed in his eyes. 'I bid Your Majesty a good day,' he said through gritted teeth. 'And hope the next time we meet, we will both see reason.'

―――

She was like the night; dark, fragrant, full of memories. Her gossamer blue sari twinkled with tiny gemstone studs. When she spread her arms, she looked like the star-spangled sky – distant even in her intimate nearness. Her steps were light, just a rustle on the sandy soil. Her smell – the sweet scent of Mogra and the sandalwood paste tattoos she wore – filled my senses. I had asked the guards to allow her access ever since I got her message. We had decided on a pink lotus as our rendezvous code and she, audaciously I thought, given how the meeting went, left one at my feet after the parley was over.

'I have come,' she whispered.

'To conquer?'

'To surrender,' she said, flowing into my arms, a midnight dream come alive. Wrapped in her spangled embrace, I gave into the tumult of her, rising and falling with waves of desire that swept away everything between us – disappointment, suspicion and fear. All that was left was a sweet rapture and the spent afterglow of glorious love. Afterwards we lay in each other's arms, not wanting to break the spell. I could feel her heart beat next to mine and ran my fingers down her sweat-slicked back. She arched back, allowing me to kiss her still swollen nipples and sighed.

'You are the kadal kol,' I whispered. 'Come to devour and destroy.'

She smiled, catching a piece of the moon on her face. 'But I offer only deliverance,' she said.

'Deliverance from what?' I asked.

'From the burden of your legacy,' she replied. 'You are not the person you become when you wear your crown,' she said. 'When you do, I hardly know you.'

'You like me better without my name?' I asked.

'This is the real you,' she said. 'The throne makes you forget that sometimes.'

'Maybe you don't know me that well, princess.'

She kissed my eyelids shut. 'Maybe you don't know yourself.'

I gave in to the sensation of the light brush of her lips all over my face – forehead, temples, bridge of the nose, cleft of the chin, corners of the mouth and finally the lips. 'And you,' I asked, breathless. 'Do you know yourself?'

'You want me to tell you what this is we have between us?' she asked.

'I can't make sense of it,' I said.

'Neither can I,' she replied quietly.

I smiled. 'Tell me, why does your brother not forbid this intimacy between us? How did you get away today? A lone woman, in the middle of the night, walking out of a city under siege?'

'My brother wants to make me his secret weapon,' she said, sadly.

'An assassination. Now I understand.'

'No, you don't,' she said. 'I am loyal to my brother and my city but I will not endorse adharma.'

'You're a fool then,' I chuckled. 'You can use any means, fair or foul, in war.'

She nuzzled up to me, tracing an invisible pattern on my chest. And then she said, 'Majesty, why are you here?'

I held her close, burying my face in her hair. The neat braid was now a dishevelled tangled mess, its garland of mogra a scattered heap of crushed petals on the bed.

'I promised you I'd come to Kanchi,' I said. 'I never forget my promises.'

'To learn Silambam?' she asked. 'Really? Then why starve my people and hound my city?'

'Are you here to make love to me or talk war?'

She laughed. 'Both. If you don't answer, I can always kill you.'

'Ask away then,' I said. 'I want to die a thousand times in your arms.'

'Even if my brother and cousin do agree to surrender, you cannot hold this land,' she said. 'It's too far from Magadh.'

'What makes you think I want to annex any of the kingdoms I have conquered on this digvijay?'

'Then why fight? Why blight the land with your sword?'

'All I am asking for is an atma nivedan, a sincere surrender and a small tax. I can't think of too many conquerors who demand so little.'

'But you are the greatest warrior in all of Jamvudeep. Why do you need this constant validation of your greatness?'

'It's a matter of strategy,' I said.

'Sounds like ego to me,' she replied, quietly.

'That's rich coming from you! Your half-brother's ego has brought starvation and plague to his people. Your city is dying because he can't make up his mind.'

She moved away and lifted herself on her elbows. 'I am sorry, Majesty,' she said softly. 'I am in no position to lecture you on anything. Sometimes my tongue tends to walk away with reason.'

I softened. 'We all have our reasons to do what we do, princess,' I said. 'Your ego is as hungry for moral victory as mine is for battle scars.'

'More battle scars,' she said, running her fingers down the axe and spear marks on my chest. And then, as if an idea just struck her, she looked into my eyes. 'You say you have nothing against our people. Then why cause them so much suffering? Why not settle this with a single face-to-face fight? My half-brother is infirm and Skanda is but a child. I can fight on their behalf. What do you say, Majesty? Are you up to the challenge?'

The idea intrigued me and for a moment I was tempted to test myself against her acrobatic war dance once more. But then I remembered Harisena's arched brow and all that was at stake. 'This is war, not an exhibition,' I said. 'Tell your brother to surrender or watch his people die.'

I was expecting an assassination attempt. Instead, Kanchi sent me a wedding proposal. Regent Vishnugopa came bearing rich silks and silver salvers piled high with rubies, emeralds and pearls. Their priest came with holy ash and an exquisite sandalwood idol of Chakrapani Vishnu. The rest of the court filed in deferentially behind them, bearing flowers (mostly pink lotus's I noticed), sweetmeats, coconuts and a pitcher full of rice custard payasam. Their town crier walked in last, reading out the proposal to us. 'His Highness Skanda Varman, sovereign ruler of Kanchi and beloved of the gods, wishes to welcome His Majesty to his kingdom and embrace him with respect and reverence. We look up to His Majesty and wish to use this opportunity of having him at our doorstep to turn our love for him into kinship. We would like to offer Princess Angai's hand in marriage to His Majesty and bind our two lands in eternal bonds of friendship and love. We will await His Majesty's decision on this offer and hope that he will allow us to make amends for whatever misunderstandings which may have cropped up between us.'

The unexpected announcement and the extravagant gifts left Harisena and me flabbergasted. Angai had, as usual, visited me the night before but she didn't say a word about this. Either Vishnugopa had kept his plans a secret from his sister or, what seemed more likely, Angai was playing his game for him. The timing of the proposal of course was not lost on either Harisena or me. We were more than six weeks into the siege and Kanchi had finally run out of options. The pox continued to claim lives even though not as many as earlier, and the city had run out of grain. Outside, the paddy crop stood golden and ready for harvest. My men, many of whom were of farmer stock, happily helped themselves to the rice while a hungry Kanchi watched. The people of the city were getting increasingly angry and the temples and guilds were growing impatient. Kanchi couldn't afford to hold out any more.

The final straw that broke the camel's back was news from Palakka that King Ugrasena was ready for talks. Like Kanchi, grain had run out in Palakka and its people were getting restive. Not as rich as Kanchi, Palakka's reserves were much smaller and King Ugrasena realized that unless he opened diplomatic channels, the siege could last forever. With his cousin breaking away, Vishnugopa finally stopped wringing his hands and decided to make a kinsman out of the enemy at his door.

That evening, Harisena walked into my enclosure, looking like thunder. 'The Kanchi officials are waiting for your response, sire,' he said softly. 'What shall I tell them?'

'You know perfectly well what to tell them,' I replied.

That old familiar arched brow matched the disapproval in the eyes. 'Do I, Majesty?' said Harisena.

'What do you mean?'

'Your intimacy with Angai hasn't gone unnoticed. It can't, in a battle camp, no matter how secret the rendezvous. I can understand your desire for female company but she is the enemy. Why are you encouraging her if you don't want this to go any further?'

I turned around and faced my best friend. 'Don't beat around the bush. If you disapprove, tell me why. Kanchi isn't our enemy. Today we are starving them, tomorrow, when they bend to our will, we will ally with them. So what's your point?'

Harisena looked away. And then he said, 'You can't marry her, Majesty. She's not of the blood. This isn't a marriage proposal. It is an insult.'

'What do you mean? She is Vishnugopa's half-sister, is she not?'

'Yes, but her mother was an atavic concubine unlike Vishnugopa's mother who was the queen,' said Harisena. 'She's not a pure-blood princess.'

'You know I have never been obsessed with bloodlines,' I said, irritated by Harisena's peculiar logic. 'Datta herself is not royal born. The life you're born into isn't important.

The life you make for yourself is. I believe in my sword arm and my destiny. And nothing else matters.'

I saw those long, tapering fingers press the throbbing veins at his temples. Harisena remained quiet for a while. And then he said, softly, almost under his breath. 'Think of Datta.'

'I am.'

'Are you, sire?' he asked, turning his gaze towards me, as if looking for clues to the conundrum that was my relationship with Angai. I didn't answer because I didn't know what to say. The truth was, the wedding proposal completely threw me off balance. I knew in my heart that I still loved Datta. She was a part of me, the one constant in my ever-changing world. With her, I never needed to explain myself. She understood without being told, the storms that raged inside me. She was my calm, my refuge from those storms.

Angai was the storm.

Our connection was like a fire, one stoke and it blazed into a conflagration. Every time we touched, we were seared by its heat, scorched by its all-consuming force. I couldn't deny it but I had no idea how to acknowledge it either. Angai was an elemental force that was devouring me with its savage strength. I burned for her every moment that we were together. I burned more every moment we were not.

And yet, when I closed my eyes, I saw a tear-stained smile and a jumble of curls that refused to be tamed into a braid. I had abandoned Datta and our child once. I couldn't do it again. I could fool everyone that this marriage was a diplomatic match. But Datta would know. And it would break her heart.

'Tell the Kanchi delegation that I must, regretfully, decline the offer of marriage to Princess Angai,' I told Harisena. 'And give them an ultimatum. If they don't surrender in the next two days, we go to war.'

14

Love and War

'I AM AFRAID IT'S goodbye, Majesty. Since you turned down our marriage proposal, my brother has forbidden me to meet you in private. He says he cannot allow his sister to whore herself to the enemy.' Angai sat on the edge of the bed, her eyes downcast. Gone was the fiery, feisty woman who had raced me to the ocean's edge and blinded me with her passion. She looked defeated, her shoulders slumped, her face twisted away from me.

I turned her face towards me and kissed her full, wide mouth. 'I know what that proposal was. So do you. Why do you want us to play games with each other?' I asked.

'What I feel for you is no game,' she said simply.

'Do you really want to marry me?'

'I am tempted to say yes,' she said.

'If you were less than who you are, you would, princess,' I said.

She nodded, sadly. 'If *you* were less than who you are, I wouldn't bother.'

I closed my eyes. 'Datta,' I said. 'With anyone else, she'd understand... take it as a diplomatic decision. But with you...'

Angai nodded. Then she said, 'For you, it is Datta. For me, it is my people. You cannot let her down because for you she will always come first. I cannot let my city down because for me Kanchi will always come first. You may be a glorious enemy but you are still the enemy.'

I looked away. 'My mistake,' I said. 'I forgot who you are. You never did.'

She remained quiet for a long time, as if weighing the words in her head. And then she said, 'I am not proud of it, you know. The way things turned out. When we met in Mathura, I never thought it would come to this. I enjoyed baiting you. Showing you there's still a lot you needed to learn. Challenging that cocksure veneer, that smug confidence in your own destiny. But then you came here. And my brother wanted me to use our old connection in the hopes of softening you up. He didn't expect our intimacy, but he didn't forbid it either. As long as it was a tactical weapon in his head, he didn't mind his sister sleeping with the enemy. Now that you've turned him down, he wants me to be a virtuous woman once more.'

I shrugged. 'I don't like him,' I said. 'I don't like to use someone else to fight my battles for me.'

Angai smiled. 'Greed for glory. It makes one believe the end always justifies the means. He has it too, just as you do.'

I frowned.

'Men make the biggest mistakes thinking it will buy them a footnote in the future,' she said. 'It rarely does.'

'The future is important,' I said. 'And there's nothing you cannot achieve if you believe in destiny and daring.'

Angai looked up. 'The bards may be singing about your digvijay right now but will the future you are fighting for remember you? Look around you, Majesty, scattered all over this land are writings carved into the rockface hundreds of years ago. They survived the implacable march of time. But the man who wanted to be remembered forever is slowly receding into the mists of memory.'

'Ashok Priyadarshi,' I said.

'Nothing lasts forever and there's no mistress more fickle than glory,' she replied.

'Says the one who knows a thing or two about being fickle,' I replied, rather bitterly.

Angai put her head in my lap and closed her eyes. 'My feelings have never been fickle. If they were, I would be on my way back to Pataliputra with you,' she said. 'But I am and always will be Angai of Kanchi. I cannot wish away the death and suffering you've caused my city. I cannot forget and I will not forgive.'

I bent down and kissed her forehead, taking in that smell of mogra and sandalwood that would forever remind me of her. 'You'll get your chance to avenge your people,' I said. 'The next time we meet, it will be on the battlefield.'

'If we come face to face, I promise not to kill you.' She smiled. 'I don't want people to say I killed the man who refused my hand.'

I knelt down and buried my face in her yakshi breasts, warm and throbbing with a life force as elemental as it was exhilarating. They rose and fell like the waves, drowning me in their promise.

'Come,' I whispered. 'Set me alight. For one last time, let's smoulder and glow, let's flicker and flare. Reduce to ashes everything that lies between us. Angai, my fierce flame, come and engulf me. Let us burn.'

It was our last night together. She slipped away the next morning, leaving behind only the faint fragrance of stale flowers and sandalwood on the bed. I rubbed my face in that scent, remembering the taste of our love on my body. The fire had gone out. I felt cold.

Harisena woke me up with the news we were waiting for.

'Ugrasena has surrendered, sire,' he said, looking exultant for the first time in weeks. 'Bhasma has sent word that the siege is over. They are working out the terms of the treaty as we speak. This will break Vishnugopa if nothing else does.'

He saw the look on my face and stopped short. 'I am sorry,' he said. 'It is good news, is it not? I rushed in to tell you because I thought you would want to know.'

'Yes,' I said. 'It is good news. Let's prepare for battle, Harisena. Tomorrow morning, we storm Kanchi. Tell the men – we give no quarters. We take no prisoners. We will raze this citadel of arrogance to the ground. We will dance on its ruins. We will show Vishnugopa what it means to cross swords with the greatest force in the world. We have shown him enough patience. Now, let's show him what our impatience looks like.'

A slow smile spread across Harisena's face. 'Jai Garuda,' he said.

Harisena had a simple plan for Kanchi. Our long siege had given us the opportunity to study the terrain much better than any of our earlier campaigns, so we left very little to chance this time around. Besides, with our southern allies helping us with men, animals and most importantly, firepower, we had no reason to ration our arrows or sling bolts.

'They will expect us to attack the gates but we will confound them and attack from every side,' said Harisena. 'We have enough ammunition. We will position our catapults all around the wall except the side facing the river. Then we will blitz the city into submission.'

I smiled. 'We will have our boats manning the river gate so if they try to escape from there, our snipers can pick them out, nice and clean.'

'Exactly,' said Harisena. 'They will be fighting on empty stomachs. And they will steer clear of the eastern ramparts where the plague-ridden are buried and, more frequently now I am told, simply left to die.'

'Then that wall will be the easiest to breach,' I said.

'But the pox?' asked Harisena.

'We will use our elephant corps and cavalry to storm the wall. Keep the foot soldiers away from that front. And ask the men to cover their noses and not touch any infected bodies,' I said. 'Just pummel everything – dead or alive – underfoot.'

Harisena nodded. 'So the plan is we bombard them from all sides, plug their river escape and breach the eastern wall,' he said.

'Yes, that should work,' I replied.

Harisena nodded but then hesitated. I caught the demur and asked, 'What is it? You've never hesitated to ask questions before.'

Harisena looked embarrassed. 'You'll meet Princess Angai on the battlefield tomorrow, Majesty,' he said. 'Our scouts brought us news that she intends to lead the charge along with their senapatis.'

'I know,' I said.

Harisena looked at me quizzically. 'And...' he trailed off.

'On the battlefield, she's the enemy,' I said simply.

'It's going to be a bloody encounter,' said Harisena. 'The Kanchi troopers have taken a blood oath, I am told. They will fight till death tomorrow.'

'At least someone is showing some courage even if their precious regent is not,' I said.

The next day dawned bright and clear, the sky was an unspoiled blue, the sea a shimmering ripple of calm. Harisena had positioned our catapults through the night and at first light the bombarding began. Boom! The shots hit home, exploding the early dawn serenity into a thousand smithereens. The blasts drowned out the twittering of the sparrows, the shrill cries of the jungle babbler and the lovelorn calls of the cuckoo – the otherwise everyday sounds that filled the air at daybreak. Instead, screams filled the air, elephants trumpeted, horses whinnied, temple bells tolled madly telling the citizens that they were under attack. The smell of sizzling smoke, charred wood and burning flesh filled our nostrils. Weapons clanged and frenzied footfalls ran helter-skelter, some rushing towards the city centre to put out the fire, others charging towards the gates to mount a counter attack. Among all the mayhem, we could see the orange flames gaily leaping from tower to tower, fanned by the morning sea breeze and helped by the complete pandemonium in the city.

Boom. Boom. Boom. The catapults kept up their relentless bombarding. Before long, the city was a blazing inferno, spewing thick black smoke that hung low like a rain cloud above us. Kanchi had woken up to its worst nightmare. As the fire leapt higher and spread further through the city, the terrified citizens ran towards the southern gate facing the river. That's when our snipers, waiting mid-stream on light coracle boats, unleashed their arrow shower, felling the first crush and forcing the rest back into their blazing city. With no water from the river to put them out, the flames grew stronger and leapt higher towards the dawning sky.

For a while, the fire and the shots threw Kanchi into such disarray that apart from a few disjointed arrow showers by the rampart guards, there was no concerted counter-attack from the city troopers. Then we saw the northern gates open, slowly, labouriously, probably expecting a mad rush from our side towards the city.

I signalled my men to hold back. I had no desire to rush in and allow the rampart guards to greet us with boiling oil and boulders. It would be much better to let their cavalry charge out towards us instead. That way, we got to choose the when, where and how of the attack. We had decided on our tried and tested Garuda vyuha formation, with my horsemen forming the beak and head while the archers made up the wings. We had strewn kiluvai thorns just outside the city gates in the north. The southern side was fenced by the river, the east was the sick bed and the west had the largest body of our men camping right in front of the gates. Harisena and I had reasoned, correctly as it turned out, that when the Kanchi troopers stormed out in battle frenzy, they would choose the northern gate expecting a quick successful raid, given the smaller cavalry force stationed there. And that's exactly how it happened.

They charged out like madmen, crazed as much by fear and fury as by the poppy-seed laced milk that all warriors drink after they take the blood oath. The charge was greeted with a furious arrow shower from our Garuda wings as the cavalry beak and head pulled back, sucking the enemy in. The kiluvai thorns did a wonderful job, hobbling the horses and throwing men to the ground. As they scampered to their feet, our poisoned arrows found easy targets among men and beast, reducing them to a howling, mangled heap and turning the area into an obstacle course for those who came after them.

The second charge was even more furious. The Kanchi troopers rode out in frenzy, trampling over their own fallen men and horses, and heading straight for our waiting cavalry beak. We held on till the last minute, spears at the ready, holding rank till their horsemen rode right into the vyuha and were trapped by it. I could feel my men trembling – it's easier to rush out and take on the enemy allowing the adrenalin to drown out the fear. It's much harder to stand back, luring the enemy right into your arms.

I heard them count under their breath – seven, six, five, four, three, two, one ... WHAM. It was like being struck by lightning and for a few blinding moments of concussion, everything became a jumbled blur. When the scene slowly rearranged itself into a clearer picture, I got an idea of the hysterical bloodletting that was unfolding around me. The Kanchi troopers had rushed pell-mell into the belly of the vyuha. The first wave impaled themselves on our line of waiting spears but these were quickly jostled and trampled out of the way by the second, third and fourth wave. The fighting was frenetic and frightful. Here a sword ripped open a man's belly, there a knife dug itself into an unguarded flank, splashing blood that turned the ochre uniform a deep bloody red. Right next to me, a Kanchi trooper trying to lunge at my horse suddenly froze; too stunned to realize he had an arrow buried in his throat. He hiccupped blood and slumped on his horse spurring the animal forward, further into the impenetrable vyuha. The air stank of fear and faeces, men pounced and grabbed, pierced and pummelled, banged and battered their way in a horrific orgy of bloodlust. Screams of anguish mixed with drug-crazed war cries drowned out the sound of the conch shells and the steady thump, thump, thump of our battle drums.

My men, sane enough not to want to lose their lives, did what they do best – follow orders. They pulled back, allowing the Kanchi charge to enter the heart of the vyuha and then they attacked. Hard. Steel clanged with steel as Asi swords danced in the morning sun, the light glinting off their beautifully carved blades. Axes swirled in a tandava dance worthy of Natraaj himself, keeping pace with the deadly swipe of the Khadaga broadsword. It was one almighty crush. Eyeballs rolled. Teeth snarled. Lips curled. Spittle sprayed. Men hacked, crushed, lunged and tore at each other. The Kanchi troopers fought well. But our vyuha formation was tight enough to confuse them about the strength of our cavalry backup. Before long, they were splintered, surrounded and slaughtered. Not one of the 400 who rushed in survived. It was a glorious victory but the bloodiest one I had ever seen.

In the middle of the melee, Harisena galloped up towards me and gave the news. 'There's a breach on the eastern wall, sire,' he said.

'Excellent, I will lead the charge,' I replied.

'That's the infected area,' said Harisena. 'You can't go in there. We can't endanger your life.'

I stopped short. 'I cannot ask my men to die for me if I am not prepared to do the same for them,' I said. 'Pox or no pox, I will lead the charge.'

Harisena's face lit up with a smile as he bowed out. It was a rare smile, given how sombre my friend had turned all through this storm-battered, fever-infested southern campaign. The old banter that kept me company in Mathura had all but disappeared here. Harisena looked care-worn and weary, as if he was fighting against his will. I knew he was against my idea of the digvijay and felt I had chosen the worst possible time given Datta's condition. Also, since these southern monarchs, unlike the Nagas, had neither rebelled nor molested us in any way, he didn't see my logic in forcing them to bend to the Garuda protection. He wasn't convinced in the war councils in Pataliputra and the year-long campaign did nothing to make him change his mind. Worse, he was completely if silently against my intimate relationship with Angai. As young men, Harisena and I had enjoyed enough romps in the courtesan quarters of Apara for him to shrug away any feminine company I may have sought out for myself during the campaign. But Angai was no faceless harlot procured for the occasional night of pleasure. Harisena resented my closeness with her, struggled to make sense of it, and blamed me for the heartbreak he knew it would cause Datta. I could see he missed the old me and the open friendship of equals that we had once shared. He couldn't trust my judgment when it came to Angai and didn't know how much it would impact my judgment with regard to Kanchi. In his mind, I was slowly turning into a stranger. But, on the eve of this bloody battle, he was simply glad to get his old friend back.

I charged towards the eastern gate, galloping into a scene of unbelievable destruction. The ground beneath was a pile of flesh and bones. Torn limbs, crushed skulls, spilled intestines, mauled bodies lay strewn all over, some dead, some dying. The ground had turned into a slushy bog under the feet of our elephant and cavalry corps. Kanchi's brown-red earth had turned a deeper shade of crimson.

The severed heads and impaled bodies of the rampart guards told me Kanchi had not expected an attack on this wall and was probably relying on the pox to keep us away. The small company of rampart guards stationed there had been taken by surprise as our elephants and horsemen burst through and it had been a pointlessly one-sided slaughter – as quick as it was brutal. Flies already buzzed around the bloodied heads and trunks and I was thankful for the turban cover on my nose which helped keep the stench at bay.

I spurred my horse towards the heart of the city, taking in the devastation caused by the catapult bolts. Here and there, the slow burning thatch on the huts that had been reduced to rubble was still spewing black smoke. The streets were deserted as we rode through, houses and shops on either side damaged first by the fire and later the elephant charge. What hadn't crumbled had been set ablaze. Here and there we saw stray signs of the struggle – a broken toy cart lying forlornly by the road, glass bangles crushed under horse hooves, torn garlands still hanging by a thread on doorways burnt to cinders, the rice flour Kolam patterns at doorsteps half-wiped out by frightened footsteps leaving behind just a smudged impression on the ground.

At first glance it looked like there was no more life remaining in the city. Then I saw her, picking her way carefully through the debris, a scrawny figure surrounded by devastation. She couldn't have been more than five or six summers old. Covered in dust and soot, her wild curls were tied into two scraggly plaits and her nervous eyes flitted from face to face looking for a reason to run. I cupped my hands to my mouth and called out, 'Come closer, little one. Don't be afraid. We won't hurt you.'

She hesitated for a moment and then walked up. I saw a small oval face, grime and tear-stained, and two large fear-filled eyes trying hard not to cry. Suddenly this nameless child reminded me of Datta as she was when I first met her, a terrified motherless child in a palace full of whispers. Her cold fingers had wrapped themselves over mine and held on. Was this child looking for a hand to hold?

I slid off the horse and knelt down in front of her. 'Are you lost, little one?' I asked.

She shook her head slowly, looking dazed, as if she had no idea where she was or what was happening around her.

'Where's your family?'

'At home,' she said simply.

'And where's home?' I asked.

She pointed to what must have once been a mud-and-brick house. It was now a heap of rubble, angry flames still licking the thatch roof that had come crashing to the ground.

'Trapped underneath?' I asked.

She nodded.

I motioned a few of my men towards the wreckage. 'See if you can dig them out,' I ordered. 'Hurry. They could still be alive.'

I saw a flash of confused resentment in their eyes. They were soldiers after all. Offering relief to the enemy wasn't something they were used to doing. Why try to save those we'd worked so hard to kill?

I turned towards the little girl. 'You mustn't wander outside, little one,' I told her.

'Why?' she asked.

'There's a big fight going on and you could get hurt.'

Suddenly her eyes filled up with tears and I could see the tiny body trembling. 'But I am scared. I can't find her. She must be lost,' she whimpered.

'Who are you looking for?' I asked.

'Kutty,' she said.

'Your sister?'

She looked at her dusty toes and shook her head. 'My parrot. She flew away when the fireball hit our home.'

'She will come home when things become quieter,' I said.

'But our home is gone,' said the child. 'She won't know where to return to.'

I looked away, not knowing what I could say to make her feel better and not wanting to meet her gaze. I wasn't squeamish about war. Like all warriors I thought of it as nasty but necessary. I didn't enjoy the killing, but I had never had a problem explaining its rationale to myself. But this scrawny child looking for her pet bird had done what years of hard fighting could not. Suddenly none of what we were doing made sense to me any more. I had brought a proud and beautiful city to its knees, but it didn't feel right this time. I looked around and saw confused impatience on the faces of my men. I let go of the little girl and pulled myself up.

'If I see her, I will send your bird back to you,' I said.

She looked up at me, her eyes filled with despair. Then she turned around and walked back to the burning thatch under which her childhood now lay buried. Suddenly, my meticulously planned battle game, the great southern digvijay, all the highs and lows of our campaign, all of it seemed utterly futile. All that really mattered was that the child found her pet bird in a city that had seen so much death that it no longer cared about living.

I rode away from my conscience towards the heart of the city where, on the palace grounds, Vishnugopa had gathered the last of his remaining city troopers for one final face-off. This was a symbolic gesture at best. The city had fallen. Its people had fled our invading army by slipping out of the breach in the walls. They hid in the paddy fields to the north and west, or the coconut groves beyond, waiting for their regent to accept defeat. The once-bustling Kanchi now looked deserted. As we galloped down the narrow brick-lined streets and turned a corner, we came upon a small public square, occupied by what looked like a 100 of our imperial guards, their ochre uniforms sweat- and blood-stained from battle. They were crowding around something or someone. Curious, I closed in for a better view. And that's when I saw her.

Angai.

She was fighting on foot and without her sword. Her armplates were gone, her breastplate shattered, rhythm broken. She looked tired from exhaustion and the loss of blood. She was simply fending off the circle of attackers with her whiplash and staff. Without her sword, she couldn't attack and they were too many anyway. My men had made a circle around her, jeering at her, calling her names. 'Witch. Whore,' they screamed. She seemed not to notice or care, keeping away the baying of the enemy with her blinding whiplash. Still acrobatic, still fierce, still fighting.

In the middle of that hubbub, I managed to catch her eye. She looked straight at me for a moment, as if willing for me to intervene. But just as I leaned forward to spur my horse towards the melee, I saw the tilt of her head. Gentle. Almost unnoticed. As if she half-agreed but not quite. Her eyes repeated the message. 'Go,' they said. 'I don't need you to fight my battle for me.'

I held her gaze for a moment more and then pulled up the reins. My horse whinnied. I turned away and galloped towards Harisena and back into the heart of the battle, leaving Angai to her fate.

We rode into what, at first glance, looked like a stampede. The palace grounds crawled with soldiers, the ochre uniforms of my men contrasting with the bright red of the Kanchi royal guards. There was furious fighting going on all around me. I saw Harisena in one corner, wielding his heavy Parashu battle axe with both hands, leaving a deadly trail of dismembered limbs and decapitated heads around him. Vishnugopa was at the other end of the melee, swinging his sword and metal whip with dazzling speed as he took on the commander of my infantry corps, General Ananta Varman's younger brother, Kuber Varman. A light-footed and athletic man, Kuber was doing a quick-step dance around Vishnugopa, staying just outside the reach of his hissing sword blade and teasing him with his own *Asi* tip. Although a formidable warrior, he was not used to the acrobatics that years of Silambam practice would have earned Vishnugopa. As a result, Kuber's nicks seldom came home to hurt and Vishnugopa was fast clearing the space around him of ochre uniforms to prepare the grounds for a face-to-face confrontation.

My first impulse was to use my long bow and simply take Vishnugopa out. I disliked the man thoroughly and with him gone, this bloodshed would also come to an immediate end. But then I realized what such an intervention would do to my reputation. Stealth kill is adharma, particularly when a man is busy fighting someone else. It reeked of cowardice. The more honourable option would be to intervene in full view. I spurred my horse ahead, inching towards the belly of the battle through crashing sword blades, hissing spear throws, bare-knuckle fist fights, colliding shields , grunts and groans, screams and swears. I emerged on Kuber's side just in time. Vishnugopa's swinging whiplash had already wrapped itself around Kuber's wrist, loosening the grip on his Asi. One tug and Kuber would be on the ground, ready to receive the edge of Vishnugopa's sword blade.

'Let him go,' I bellowed. 'You want to show us how well you fight? Come, take me on then!'

I saw his grey eyes glint. 'I bested him,' said Vishnugopa through gritted teeth. 'He will die.'

'You kill him, I kill you,' I said quietly. 'Your city has fallen. Your troopers are dead. Your people have fled. If this is about honour, let's fight honourably.'

'You taught us there's no honour in war,' said Vishnugopa.

'You're right,' I said. 'I am wasting my time.' Before he could react, my Asi swished through the air and gashed a deep scratch on his wrist and fist. The unexpected attack gave him a jolt, a moment's break in his concentration, enough for me to yank the metal whip out of his hand. Kuber, still trembling at how close he had come to death, quickly released himself from its grip and dropped to my feet, mumbling his gratitude. 'Leave,' I said to him quietly.

Vishnugopa's eyes blazed with anger.

'We should have done this a long time ago,' he said.

I didn't reply. I had my trusted Asi in one hand and the Khadaga broadsword in the other. 'Come,' I said. 'Let's play.'

For a while, we circled each other, Vishnugopa swirling his short sword and cracking his metal whip, trying to gauge a break in my defence while I tried to take in his rhythm and figure how best to block the unusual angle of his sword thrust. He attacked first, pirouetting prettily before unleashing the double lash of the metal whip as well as his short sword, one trying to lasso my sword arm, the other trying to find a gap in my flank to bury itself into. I remembered my lessons with Angai and used my sword to block those unusual angles. One, two, three. I saw surprise in his eyes. Vishnugopa had entirely miscalculated my ability to take on the speed and acrobatics of his Silambam-inspired moves. He pulled back and then returned for more.

This time, he somersaulted; neatly landing just before me on the ground so that the sword thrust would be from an angle below. Once again, I remembered my lessons and used the Asi to parry, pulling back to give myself enough space to use the Khadaga. Vishnugopa, realizing how vulnerable that left his neck, rolled away and quickly sprung back on his feet.

Round three. This time I attacked, unleashing my quicksilver thrusts to force Vishnugopa to fight conventionally, not giving him the time to use his acrobatics to break my rhythm. Hack. Hack. Hack. My Asi hissed in the air nicking his forearms and neck, forcing him to pull back to catch his breath. I saw a look of wariness in his eyes – Vishnugopa had no idea I knew Silambam. And without the novelty of his martial art, he was no match for me in brute strength or stamina.

Round four. I rushed in, swirling the Khadaga broadsword. Beloved of Yama, the God of Death, the Khadaga is a deadly weapon when yielded with the right amount of force and at the right angle. Broader and heavier than the Asi, it can shatter smaller swords and cleanly decapitate a man in the blink of an eye. Hack. Hack. Hack. Once again, I was too quick for Vishnugopa to try his tumbling and pirouetting. As he saw the Khadaga swish in the air, he pulled back in alarm, just in time for the blade to neatly slice through his breastplate, exposing his torso to its lethal lick.

'A broadsword to take on a whipcord?' shouted Vishnugopa. 'How's that a fair fight?'

I shrugged. 'Drop one of your weapons and I will do the same,' I said.

Vishnugopa dropped his metal whip. He realized that without his Silambam moves, the metal whip would not be as effective as a sword. I let the Khadaga drop to the ground and saw relief flood his eyes. His shorter sword against my Asi was, to him, as level a field as it could get. What Vishnugopa didn't know was though I could use both hands to wield a weapon, I was in fact left-handed. So my thrusts would come at an angle he would find very difficult to block.

Round five. I allowed Vishnugopa to return to position and then rushed in with full force. I saw the surprise in his eyes as I moved the Asi from my right hand to my left, and moments later I was angling a flurry of lunges that each targeted his now exposed flank. The blows came down at him from left to right, which meant that his left flank was left unprotected by the sword in his right hand. Vishnugopa clumsily blocked the first couple of slashes but the speed and the angle were disturbing his weapon's rhythm. My Asi hovered around his left flank, making him focus on defence rather than attack. Five, six, seven, eight, nine … On the tenth thrust, the Asi tip found the flank it was looking for and dug in. Vishnugopa flinched in terror, giving me time to retrieve my weapon and come back for his jugular. He saw the Asi tip sail through the air and tried to lean away from its tongue. Unfortunately, he stumbled on his own metal whip and fell backwards, twisting his sword arm in the process. I walked over and held the tip of my Asi at his throat.

For what seemed like an eternity, Vishnugopa held my gaze. And then, slowly, he lowered his eyes.

'Had enough?' I asked.

The grey eyes looked away as if trying to take in the destruction all around. Then he looked up to meet my gaze. The thin lips stayed pursed for a moment more and then he murmured the words I wanted to hear.

'I humbly offer atma nivedan to your Garuda protection, Your Majesty,' he said. 'I swear I shall always be a loyal ally to the empire.'

I turned around to bump straight into Harisena. There was no arch on my best friend's brow. Harisena looked me straight in the eye and said, 'It's Princess Angai. She's surrounded.'

I looked at Vishnugopa, still slumped on the ground next to his weapons. 'Don't worry about him,' whispered Harisena. 'Go. Before it's too late.'

I jumped on my horse and galloped through that seething, teeming, raving mass of men, holding my Garuda pennant aloft for my men to see and pull back, allowing me to ride through.

I heard the howls first. My men sounded like a pack of jackals, bloodthirsty and maddened with hunger. She was hobbling, her armour shattered, her metal whip flung to a far corner, her clothes torn. She was covered in scratches and there was a deep gash on her right thigh. Her forearms were bloodied and her once blindingly swift movements were now slow and heavy, as if draining her of whatever energy was left in that lithe body.

'Stop,' I shouted. 'I command you.'

In that tumult, my voice had been drowned. The circle was closing in on her. The mob screamed and jeered, laughed and poked her with their swords and spears. She tried to fend off the attacks, in vain. There were just too many of them. I saw the panic in her eyes. Meenakshi, I liked to call them, unblinking like those of a fish. The blades pushed and prodded, making her jerk and flail her Kampu staff, the only weapon she had left. And then it happened.

I watched in horror as a spear flew through the air in slow motion and buried itself in her belly. She stumbled and fell. I spurred my horse into that bloody circle, half-crazed with grief and rage. I slid off the horse and ran full tilt into the still baying crowd, my sword unsheathed. 'Stand back,' I roared. 'Anyone who touches her is a dead man.'

My men moved back, surprised, frightened to see their emperor rushing in. I pulled out the spear with one big heave and used my uttaria scarf to tightly bandage her abdomen. She groaned and licked her cracked lips. I lifted her up and carried her to my horse. She slumped against me and sighed, almost relieved. I held on to her tightly so she wouldn't slide off the horse but she turned limp in my arms. Her head lolled forwards. Her warm skin, which once breathed fire into my soul, was now cold and clammy. Her breathing was shallow, laboured. I felt life draining from her. 'Don't give up,' I shouted into her ear. 'You're a warrior. Fight back.'

As I rode away from the battlefield, I heard her speak softly into my chest. 'You came back,' she said, gently smiling.

It took us several days more to hammer out the treaty that officially declared Kanchi's atma nivedan to the Garuda banner. Angai remained in bed all through though she slowly regained strength with each passing day. By the time we were ready to leave, she could sit up when I dropped by to visit. We walked on eggshells around each other, talking about this and that – the weather, the rice payasam that Harisena had acquired a taste for, my Silambam practice and my daily trips to the ocean's edge.

'For someone who has grown up surrounded by land, you sure are the Ocean's Own,' she joked.

'I close my eyes and all I see is a blue eternity,' I said.

Angai laughed. 'As you should, Maharaja Adhiraja Samrat Sri Samudragupta. Destroyer of kings. Ruler of the world. *Prithivim Avitva Divam Jayatya Prativarya Virya* (king of kings, ruler of heaven and earth, protector of all four realms).'

I laughed, not wanting to talk of the destruction and bloodshed that had come with that title, not knowing what to say that wouldn't hurt either of us. I was leaving Kanchi a ghost of its former self. I couldn't forget what we'd done any more than she could forgive.

Then she said, 'You must write it in stone. So people won't forget. That there was once a man who wanted to own the ocean. And it ended up owning him instead.'

I smiled. 'Tell your tale in stone,' she continued. 'It will survive long after our memories have died.'

I looked away and saw Harisena patiently waiting for me at the doorway. He caught my eye and smiled. No more arched brows – my best friend was just happy to be going back to where we belonged. Away from the ocean. Away from Angai.

I turned back to her and saw her staring at the bright, cloudless sky through the window. I watched her profile silhouetted against that unspoiled blue and closed my eyes to sear the moment in my head. Years later, the memory of that proud head outlined in shadow against a brilliant patch of sky, was all I could remember of our last few moments together. That, and the lingering smell of Mogra and sandalwood.

'I don't think we will meet again, Princess,' I said. 'Not unless your brother and nephew get ideas in their head about just how serious I am when it comes to the letter and spirit of the atma nivedan.'

'My kinsmen may be proud but they are not suicidal,' she replied quietly. 'They know what you expect. They won't risk having you back at our doorstep again.'

I nodded. Suddenly there were no more words left between us. I stared at my sword hilt and wondered how to say goodbye. When I looked up, I met her calm, unblinking, Meenakshi gaze.

'If you were any less the man you are,' she said softly, 'I would beg you to take me with you.'

'If you were any less the woman you are,' I replied, 'I would beg you to come with me.'

EPILOGUE—365 AD
A Future in the Stones

SOMETIMES MEMORIES PLAY TRICKS on us. The moments that we thought would live forever fade away, like colours draining from a painting. And all we are left with is a faint whiff of forgetfulness.

It's been thirty years since my digvijay. I never went back to Kanchi. I never met Angai again. She became the unspoken name between Datta and myself, and in time I could no longer recall the details of that proud, fierce face. But every now and then, a sudden flash of cerulean blue would bring back memories. Of a conquest and a surrender. And my nose would fill with the fragrance of Mogra and sandalwood.

I am no longer a young man. When I think back and remember, I wonder if things really happened the way they did. And then I remember the pillar. It is all cast in stone, I tell myself.

It was Harisena who found the pillar in the Kosala capital of Koshambi – one of Ashok Priyadarshi's stone messages, beautifully carved and in almost pristine condition. I didn't mind sharing posterity with him. This blessed land that I now claim as mine belonged to many before and will belong to many after me. What better way to celebrate that continuity than through a link with the past carved in stone for the future?

Men and memories fade away. Time draws a shroud over both glory and ignominy. But my story, I know, will beat this inexorable oblivion. My story will survive. Long after I have gone.

For I am Maharaja Adhiraja Samrat Sri Samudragupta. Destroyer of kings. Ruler of the world. *Prithivim Avitva Divam Jayatya Prativarya Virya.*

I am the Ocean's Own.

More than sixteen centuries later, the Prayag Pillar with Harisena's prasasthi of Samudragupta still stands. More than a millennia after Kacha left his imprint on the Ashokan pillar, another monarch did the same – Mughal Emperor Jahangir. History truly has a way of joining the dots for posterity.

THE END

About the Author

Nandini Sen Gupta is a Pondicherry-based journalist and author of historical fiction and narrative history. After a chance visit to Ajanta Ellora caves, she became fascinated with India's past in general and ancient India in particular. For the next ten years, she read history for fun. Her book credits include the bestselling *The Blue Horse And Other Amazing Animals from Indian History* (Hachette), which debuted in November 2020, *The King Within* and *The Poisoned Heart*, Books I and II of the Gupta Empire Trilogy by HarperCollins Publishers India and *The Story of Kalidas: The Gem Among Poets* by Eicher Goodearth Publications.

The Ocean's Own is the third and final book in the Gupta Empire Trilogy. Nandini is currently writing her first narrative non-fiction biography to be published in 2022.